"We both said things we regret."

"I sure did. I'm sorry."

"It's okay. I think we're good now." She looked across the creek, and for a minute the only sounds were Roscoe slurping from the creek and the jangling of his tag. "We both have our reasons for passionately fighting for that storefront."

"Is there another reason you want that space? Something I should know about?"

He expected a quick denial, but instead she sighed. "Nothing big, no."

"But something."

She nodded. "Something."

At that moment, he wanted to be there for her. To support her. To be her friend.

Something he hadn't felt with a woman in a long, long time.

His parents wouldn't like it, but there was nothing wrong with being friends with a woman. Even if it was a woman like Faith, whose heart was even prettier than her features. He wouldn't mess up.

"Tell me, Faith. What am I missing?"

Susanne Dietze began writing love stories in high school, casting her friends in the starring roles. Today she's blessed to be the author of over half a dozen historical romances. Married to a pastor, and mom of two, Susanne loves fancy-schmancy tea parties, cozy socks and curling up on the couch with a costume drama and a plate of nachos. You can find her online at www.susannedietze.com.

Books by Susanne Dietze

Love Inspired

A Future for His Twins

Love Inspired Historical

The Reluctant Guardian
A Mother for His Family

A Future
for His Twins

Susanne Dietze

LOVE INSPIRED
INSPIRATIONAL ROMANCE

LOVE INSPIRED®

INSPIRATIONAL ROMANCE

Recycling programs
for this product may
not exist in your area.

ISBN-13: 978-1-335-48863-3

A Future for His Twins

Copyright © 2020 by Susanne Dietze

This edition published by arrangement with Harlequin Books S.A.

For questions and comments about the quality of this book,
please contact us at CustomerService@Harlequin.com.

Love Inspired
22 Adelaide St. West, 40th Floor
Toronto, Ontario M5H 4E3, Canada
www.Harlequin.com

Printed in U.S.A.

But seek ye first the kingdom of God,
and his righteousness; and all these things
shall be added unto you.
—*Matthew* 6:33

For Hannah, whose spark lights up our lives.
I'm so glad God made me your mom.

Chapter One

Faith Latham had downed her usual portion of morning caffeine, but it was adrenaline, pure and simple, that made her hands shake when she locked the door to her antiques store.

She'd waited months for this moment, and now she was about to march to city hall and submit the rental application. In a matter of days, she'd be the proprietor of not one but two businesses on historic Main Street in her hometown of Widow's Peak Creek, California—her antiques store and a town museum.

She didn't normally whoop in public, but she did now. Nobody was around to hear anyway at this early hour. The other shops didn't open until ten o'clock.

She hadn't gone more than a few steps when she paused to peer through the dusty window next door, cupping her hands around her eyes to block the glare. Her brief touch left a thick layer of sooty grime on her hands. Ugh. She couldn't submit her rental application with smudges, now could she? Thankfully she always carried moistened wipes in her purse.

Mid-scrub, Faith noticed a black SUV pull into one of the parking spots right in front of her.

At quarter after nine, it was early in the day for tourists, so she stayed put in case they wanted into her store. She'd direct them to the café or bakery down the street and invite them to come back at ten o'clock.

A man in dark rinse jeans and a well-worn leather jacket emerged from the driver's side, only to turn around and open the back door behind him. He reached in, as if retrieving packages.

Or a child. A small boy with dark hair ducked under the man's arm and hopped up to the sidewalk. The man stood to his full height and backed away, allowing a second child, a girl this time, out of the vehicle. A large yellow dog leaped out after her.

It was always good to see families spending time together in town, but when a woman appeared from the passenger seat, it became obvious this was no family of four. The shade of platinum blond hair and fashionable cut of her periwinkle blue blazer could belong to no one but Judy Hughes, mayor of Widow's Peak Creek. Stepping around the large dog as if afraid to touch it, Mayor Hughes withdrew a key.

Faith's stomach sank to her ballet flats.

"Oh, hello, Faith." Mayor Hughes's stiffening shoulders caused her blazer's shoulder pads to rise.

"Good morning, Mayor." Faith was about to extend an obligatory greeting for the tall man alongside her when his dark gaze met hers and recognition hit her square in the solar plexus. His black wavy hair was longer now, tousled and pushed away from his face, and he clearly hadn't shaved in a few days. The overall look wasn't the least bit disheveled, though. On the contrary, the scruffy look suited him. He was as handsome as he'd been back in high school when she, a lanky, gawky nerd then, noticed him from afar.

She might forever be a nerd, in some people's minds anyway, but she was no longer an awkward adolescent. She thrust out her hand. "Tomás Santos? It's good to see you again."

"I'm sorry, you have me at a disadvantage." His hand was warm, enveloping hers in a firm shake. "But we've obviously met. Call me Tom."

"We attended high school together. Faith Latham."

"Latham." Now that the handshake was over, he snapped his fingers. "Chloe's little sister."

Yep. That was Faith, all through her growing-up years. Sister to the far more outgoing Chloe, the cheerleader. Or she was sometimes Chloe's "smarter" sister, when *smart* was the total opposite of being *in*, because Faith aced all the history quizzes.

Tom Santos, however, had been a whiz at everything from soccer to art. Two years older than Faith, he'd left for college, married and then been widowed, according to town chatter. Apparently, he returned on occasion to visit his parents. But if he was here with the mayor, looking at a vacant storefront, he was in Widow's Peak Creek for something more permanent.

Which was fine, of course. Just not in *this* building. It was hers.

Unless he was a contractor or architect or something here to evaluate the historic building's integrity. That would be okay. Nevertheless, Faith stayed fixed in her position, guarding the doors while the mayor withdrew a key. "Looking at the old livery, Mayor Hughes?"

"Is that what this place used to be?" Tom leaned back,

taking in the story-and-a-half height, the pale yellow siding and the white-trimmed windows. "Okay, I can see it now. The wide doors, high ceilings to accommodate carriages and a hayloft back in the old days, right? It'll be perfect for my outdoor gear store."

Oh, no, it wouldn't. It wouldn't be good for anything but her museum, and it was too bad he wasn't a contractor like she'd hoped, because she was about to wreck his day.

Faith dug the rental application out of her purse. "Here you go, Mrs. Hughes. As we discussed."

The mayor couldn't possibly have forgotten those discussions, right? About Faith waiting for Leonard, the proprietor of the knickknack store that used to be here, to retire so she could rent the space? And then they'd talked again after Leonard announced his retirement and bought a house in Oregon. Faith had informed the mayor she'd be ready with the rental application on the first day the store was deemed available. Faith had been clear as the sweet water that flowed through the creek about her intentions, so why on earth was the mayor showing the property to someone else as if she were a real estate agent?

Faith's stomach soured. The rumors about the mayor were true. Judy Hughes wanted to shift the town's focus in a different direction, from a historic district to something she deemed more lucrative. She didn't want Faith's museum in this storefront. She wanted something like Tom's store—*outdoor gear*, he'd said. That would certainly explain why she studiously avoided taking the paperwork from Faith.

Tom's gaze caught on the black-lettered sign hanging from the underside of the white wood balcony next door.

Her balcony, attached to the apartment above the store that she shared with her cat.

"*Faith's Finds*. That's you? Antiques store?" At her nod, he smiled and took another look at the facade, white paint, seafoam green wood chairs set outside with a wrought iron café table between them. "Looks like we'll be neighbors."

Faith glanced at his kids. The boy clung to Tom's knee, and the girl kept her hand on the dog as it sniffed the concrete sidewalk. They might not be listening, but the last thing she wanted was to upset them, so she'd need to choose her words and tone with care.

"Actually, Tom, I'll be renting this storefront and expanding my business. It's arranged."

"The building isn't available?" His head snapped back as if he'd been slapped.

"No, and I'm sorry for the waste of your time." She truly was. This wasn't his fault. But it wasn't Faith's, either, and she'd do well not to take responsibility for things that weren't her doing. She'd had a bad habit of doing that when she was younger, and she'd worked hard to find a healthier balance. She gestured at the large doors of the old livery. "This is going to be the Widow's Peak Creek Museum, and this is the rental paperwork," she said, holding it up.

A warm, wet nudge to her hand tugged her gaze downward. The yellow dog bumped her fingers, an invitation to scratch his ears. His fur was soft but not as silky as her cat's. Then again, her cat didn't nuzzle quite like this.

"That's Roscoe," the girl said. "He's seven. And I'm six."

"I'm six, too." The boy's brown eyes stared up at Faith, his expression as cautious as his quiet voice.

The girl spun in a circle. "But I'm the little sister."

Tom's grin quirked up higher on the right than the left. "You're twins, Nora. You're younger than Logan by eight minutes."

"I'm still the baby." Nora continued twirling, making her pink-and-white-striped skirt swirl about her knees.

"At any rate." Mayor Hughes's tight tone indicated she was finished with pleasantries. "That paperwork is a *request* to rent a historic building, Faith, not a guarantee. You haven't even submitted it."

Faith's fingers chilled. She was en route to submitting it, on the very day the mayor had told her the rental application would be accepted. Arguing the point here in front of the kids wouldn't help anything, though, so she zipped her lips for the time being.

Tom's heavy brows knit. "You didn't mention there were any other interested parties, Mayor. Not this morning and not two weeks ago when you first mentioned the space."

Oh, so the mayor had been the one to tell Tom about it and had not said a word to Faith? This was getting worse and worse.

"Two weeks ago we lived in our old house," the little girl interrupted, doing some sort of dance move. "But now we have a new house on the river."

"It's a creek, not a river." Logan's voice rose, but then he glanced at Faith again and scooched behind his dad's legs.

"Anyway," the mayor said, glancing at her watch. "I didn't mislead either of you. Anyone interested in renting the property may look at it. If you both determine you want the building and file your applications within forty-eight hours of one another, you'll be invited to present your cases to the council at our next meeting if you desire."

Of course, she desired. This town needed a museum—no, it deserved one. Faith tipped up her chin. "I intend to file my application today. You should know that, Tom."

"I appreciate the heads-up, Faith. That said, this place seems perfect for my needs. If I like what I see inside, I'm going to submit an application as well, and you and I will be competing for the space."

Then he'd better be prepared to lose. She'd waited a long time for this building. She wasn't about to give up now.

The Labrador's loud snort startled Faith, and he ran past her. Tom groaned and dashed after him. Clutching her application to her chest, Faith spun around.

Her gray cat, Bettina, had somehow slipped outside, and was perching casually on one of the two seafoam green chairs she'd set in front of her store, licking a front paw. And the Santos family dog was headed straight for her.

Tom lunged for Roscoe's collar and missed. He should've leashed him. Should've—well, it didn't matter now, since his dog was *this close* to fighting with someone's cat.

"Bettina!" Faith ran past him, reaching toward the cat.

Great. *Her* cat.

The situation between them was tenuous already without his dog going after her pet. Roscoe had never bitten anything more lively than a chew toy, but there was a first time for everything.

Lord, don't let him give chase.

Tom's second attempt at gripping Roscoe's collar was

successful, mainly because Roscoe had stopped a few feet short of Faith's cat, jaw thankfully shut. The cat, to his shock, was not freaking out.

Huh.

Faith scooped up the gray fur ball. "She must have followed me outside. I usually see her if she tries to slip out but I—was in a hurry to get to city hall."

"I'm just glad there wasn't an altercation." Tom urged Roscoe back a few feet. "I'm sorry if we scared you."

"Bettina doesn't seem scared, but she's sure watching your dog."

And Roscoe was watching her back, with a gentle gaze and his tongue lolling out.

Nora, a lover of all things fluffy, materialized at Faith's side. "May I pet your cat?"

"Her name's Bettina. She likes gentle strokes on top of her head, here between her ears." Faith bent at the knees so Nora could reach easier. "You're doing a great job."

Logan, far more cautious than his sister, patted Tom's pant leg. "Is the cat purring?"

It was practically a whisper, but Logan was shy when it came to being around new people. At least, he had been since his mom died. Trying to encourage Logan to join his sister, Tom tipped his chin at the cat. "I can't tell from here."

As if she understood, Faith carried the cat to Logan. "She's not purring right now, but she's probably feeling a little cautious. You can still pet her if you want."

Logan's hand snaked out and patted the cat's sleek back.

"Maybe later when she's comfortable, you can pet her and I'm sure she'll purr for you. Sometimes she sounds like a motorboat."

The kids giggled. Faith might be put out with the mayor—and him, probably—but at least she was nice to his kids.

Odd he hadn't remembered her on sight, but her hair was different, shorter now with loose dark blond waves that fell to her shoulders. Her bearing seemed different, too. He recalled a shy skinny kid back in high school burdened by a stuffed backpack and carrying even more books in her arms. But now she stood straight and tall—and not just because she held a cat instead of half a library. Something had certainly changed with Faith Latham since he'd seen her last. Like she'd come into her own somehow.

"Folks?" Mayor Hughes called their attention back to the vacant business. She waved her cell phone in the air. "I've got to get back to city hall, so if you want to look inside, Mr. Santos?"

"Let me get a leash on this guy first. Kids, stay on the sidewalk." He guided Roscoe to the back of the car, pressing buttons on his key fob. The hatchback lifted and Tom yanked the red leash from a mesh bag in the back. By the time he finished clipping it to Roscoe's collar, the mayor had pushed the door open and Faith was striding inside, Nora's hand practically glued to the cat's head as she walked alongside.

Why did Faith have to come in now, when he wanted to see things for himself? Was she trying to further her nonexistent claim on the place?

A place that a few months ago he'd never considered occupying to run a store. In a town he never thought he'd live in again, after he'd left twelve years ago.

Was he really doing this? Returning to the Sierra Nevada Foothills to start over?

As a kid, he wanted to escape small-town life. He attended college in San Francisco and loved the change of pace. He met Lourdes, married her and started a career in advertising. He'd been so good at his job he'd been given extra responsibilities—which paid well but kept him working many evenings and weekends. Most wives would have complained, but not Lourdes. She'd appreciated the financial security he provided. It was her priority as much as it was his.

He'd thought their life was ideal. Until last year, when Lourdes suffered an aneurysm one morning after dropping the kids off at preschool. No warning, nothing anyone could have done. Yet, it threw their lives into a tailspin.

Stop it. Not now, not here.

Tom swallowed down the all too familiar lump in his throat and stepped inside the vacant building, forcing his attention to focus on the moment…and the future. He had kids to provide for, and this was the best way to do it. So would this building work for his store?

The dimensions seemed right. He liked the airiness of it, as well as the look, with rustic wooden beams on the ceiling, and the north wall made up of exposed river rock.

The mayor flipped on the lights, setting overhead fluorescents flickering. They would definitely need replacing with LEDs. Maybe brushed nickel track lighting, mounted in such a way as to complement the ceiling beams rather than compete with them.

The mayor noted the direction of his gaze and gestured at the beams as if she were a game show hostess showing off a prize display. "They're original, but decorative now, of course. The twenty properties on this section of Main Street are original to the town's founding in

1852 and by city charter must maintain their authenticity as historic sites, but that doesn't mean the buildings are dilapidated or uncomfortable in any way. Everything is safe and sturdy, compliant with state and local codes."

A touch of the building's original charm balanced with modern conveniences and security. Perfect. "Flooring looks good."

"Come see the rest," the mayor invited.

Faith followed along, uninvited but quiet. They toured the office in the back and a larger space that would make an ideal break room for employees. The restrooms were clean, if not as modernized as he'd hoped. Perhaps he could make a few changes, but otherwise?

This place was perfect. Well, almost. "Smells a little musty in here. Mildew?"

"Assuredly not." The mayor blinked at the suggestion.

Faith walked past them. "The building's been closed up for a few weeks so the air is stagnant. Baking soda and vinegar will freshen up the place." She paused to stare at the south-facing wall at—nothing that Tom could see.

What was she looking at? If there was a problem, an imperfection or issue, he needed to know. Immediately. "Is something wrong?"

Faith shifted her cat into the crook of her left arm so she had a free hand to trace a line on the wall. "See this crack here? It's faint because it's been painted over."

Tom couldn't see anything from ten feet away, but Nora stopped patting the cat's head to rub the wall. Logan, who'd been by Tom's side the entire tour, inched closer and stuck his fingernails into what must be a seam in the paint.

"I feel it, Dad."

That didn't sound good.

Faith was smiling, though. "This was—is, actually— a door connecting this building to the store next door. The owners of the original buildings were cousins, and this space was a livery, where horses and buggies were rented out. The store on the other side sold animal feed and seeds, but now it's my store, Faith's Finds. I'd like to open the door again to connect the buildings."

"What's in Faith's Finds?" Nora poked the wall as if she could push through and enter the antiques store.

"Old things," Tom answered before Faith could.

"That's one way of looking at it." She glanced back at him as if disappointed.

"I didn't mean to sound dismissive of your business. Sorry."

"But you don't like antiques, I take it. That's all right. Tastes differ."

The last antique couch he'd sat on was lumpy and hard. Plop on that every day to watch sports? No, thanks. He preferred his year-old leather sofa and matching love-seat and recliners. But that wasn't the point. As far as he was concerned, other people could enjoy vintage stuff all they wanted—in her store.

This building, though, was Tom's future. It was personal for him. Surely, once Faith heard his side of things—that he was doing this for his children and to invest in the town where he'd grown up—she'd relent.

And if she didn't?

He would do whatever he could to get this building, even if it set him at odds with his new next-door neighbor. He could endure a lifetime of Faith Latham's resentment, if it meant stability and peace for his children.

Chapter Two

Faith appreciated the tour of the shop, even if it hadn't been intended for her. She hadn't been inside the space since it was last occupied by Leonard's gift shop, decked floor to ceiling with candles, wind chimes, postcard racks and knickknacks. Now that she could view the bare walls and floor, she had a better idea of what she would need to do when she set up her museum here.

She'd seen enough, though. She turned back to the mayor and Tom. "Thank you for allowing me to look."

The mayor's stern expression was a stark reminder Faith hadn't really been invited in the first place.

"We're finished, too." Tom gathered his children and followed Faith outside.

Mayor Hughes locked the door behind them. "Remember, if you both submit applications within two days, you'll be invited to present proposals to city council at our meeting on the sixteenth."

Less than two weeks to come up with a proposal? Faith gulped. That was hardly any time at all.

"That's plenty of time." Tom grinned.

Oh, yeah. He'd been on the debate team in high school, hadn't he? Great.

Tom shook the mayor's hand and nudged the children to do the same. The mayor didn't give Faith a chance at a handshake, however, ignoring Faith's extended hand and rushing off north in the direction of city hall.

Huh. The mayor might not like history the way Faith did, but some things never went out of style. Like common courtesy.

Faith decided she should probably follow after Mayor Hughes and submit her rental application at city hall before it was time to open her store. "Nice to see you again, Tom, and to meet you, Logan and Nora. Roscoe, too."

"Bye, kitty." Nora stroked Bettina's triangular ears. Logan looked like he wanted to pat the cat but held back.

Tom didn't say goodbye, either. Instead, his brow furrowed. "Could we discuss the situation, Faith? Maybe come to an understanding?"

One where she agreed to let him have the store? No. But maybe she could persuade *him* to back away so she could have it. Turning in the application could wait. "Sure. Why don't you come into my shop?"

"What about Roscoe?"

"Widow's Peak Creek is dog-friendly." She tipped her chin down at a water-filled stainless steel pet dish near the green chair where Bettina had sat. "You'll see bowls like this in front of several stores. Leashed dogs are welcome in most places as long as they're well-behaved."

Which explained why Bettina hadn't bolted when Roscoe got close. She was used to dogs coming around.

"The kids will be well-behaved, too." Tom exchanged loaded glances with his twins and tightened his grip on

Roscoe's leash. "I know stores like this are full of break-ables, kids, so don't touch anything."

Logan grinned. "Not even the floor with my feet?"

He was definitely the shyer of the twins, and it warmed Faith that he was thawing to her.

"Very funny, kiddo." Tom grinned back at the boy. "You know what I mean."

"Hands to ourselves." Nora folded her arms over her chest.

"Actually, there are plenty of things you can touch. I'll show you." Faith unlocked the door and pushed it open. "Welcome to Faith's Finds."

The kids tiptoed inside, as if afraid to make noise. Tom's steps were hesitant, too, and he gripped Roscoe's leash like he feared the dog would crash into a tea set. Once he cleared the threshold, though, his shoulders re-laxed. "Wow, this is nice, Faith."

"Thanks." She couldn't take credit for having a designer's eye to achieve the look of the displays, how-ever. She'd visited other antiques stores and boutiques for inspiration, but she'd been drawn most of all to the lay-outs of her favorite tea shops. Like a home with no walls, she'd grouped her wares in such a way as to resemble rooms, using decorative screens to separate the spaces, creating cozy nooks for sitting, filling vintage vases with silk floral arrangements and displaying smaller items on bookshelves.

And like a tea shop, she offered tea to her custom-ers, hot or iced depending on the season. Although she served hers in tiny paper cups, not china.

The children gaped at the area Faith lovingly called the "farmhouse," where three galvanized windmill fans hung above a scarred kitchen table. A wood-carved checkerboard waited for players. "Go ahead," she encouraged.

Tom must have felt the checkerboard was nice and safe, because he stopped hovering and wandered with Roscoe toward the Victorian bedroom furniture, to which Faith had added a hundred-year-old fireplace mantel topped with a gilt-framed mirror and sepia-tinted portraits. "This looks like a room at a bed-and-breakfast."

"I've sold pieces like this to a few hotels, including the Creekside Inn." It was the town's prettiest B&B.

"I spent years in marketing and design, and I've got to say, you've done a good job. I didn't get a look at your front window when we came in, but from the back it's inviting, too."

She'd parked a refurbished robin's-egg blue cruiser bicycle in the front window, filling the basket with dried flowers and surrounding it with potted grasses and a blue fabric kite. "Thanks. My favorite seasons with the shop windows are Christmas and autumn."

A few notes of Westminster Chimes carried faintly through the store. Uh-oh. The grandfather clock was telling her it was half past the hour, and she had a few things to do before the store opened in thirty minutes. "I'll be right back. I need to put the tea kettle on."

Not the celebratory tea she'd hoped to share with her assistant, Angie, but all hope was not lost. Nevertheless, a flutter of nerves spread from her stomach as she made her way to the tiny kitchenette at the rear of the store. She filled the large kettle with water, set it to boil and measured out loose-leaf tea into silk sachets so the beverage would be ready for customers.

If any came today. Spring weekdays were not her busiest season. If it hadn't been for that project she'd done a few months back for that boutique hotel in San Francisco, she might not have been able to pay the rent during the post-Christmas slump.

A flutter of panic spread from her stomach and quickened her pulse. Tom's interest in the old livery and the mayor's implied support of his endeavor was shaking her fragile trust in God's provision, but she mustn't allow herself to slip into fear. Despite her family's apathy and the mayor's downright disinterest in preserving the town's legacy by supporting a museum, Faith had to remember she was not alone. God was with her.

He knew the museum was her dream. She believed He'd put it into her heart, and if that was the case, she should stop staring blankly at the teakettle and put her beliefs into practice.

Lord, I'm deciding here and now to trust You with my bills and the museum. Show me what I need to do and help me to leave the rest to You.

When she returned with the large kettle, Tom and the kids were in the 1950s-era kitchen set up in the rear of the store. Logan was playing with an eggbeater and Nora had dropped to her haunches to peek into the oven. Tom flinched when he saw Faith. "Hope you don't mind. These things were down low, so I let them touch gently."

"That's fine. Nothing fragile is low enough for them to reach, except for some of the vases." Faith poured the hot water into the stainless steel urn on the tea cart, then dropped the sachet of tea leaves inside. "I want people, young and old, to experience and enjoy things from the past."

"Is that why you want to open a museum next door?"

She nodded, glad to discuss her favorite topic—and maybe persuade him to look for another site for his store.

"Since you grew up here, you know Widow's Peak Creek is a vital part of the California gold rush history. The city charter made some provisions to preserve the town heritage, like ensuring these twenty buildings on old Main Street are protected—plus a few others the mayor didn't mention, like the old church across Church Street—but so much more could be done. There's nowhere for visitors or townsfolk alike to be educated about our history. I've lobbied for a museum, but Mayor Hughes and the council repeatedly insist the town isn't in a financial position to take one on at the moment. So I decided to take matters into my own hands." Grinning, she beckoned Nora and Logan. "Kids, let me show you something."

In the shop's south corner, she'd created an exhibit on the area, complete with a glass cabinet of gold-mining tools, photographs and informative plaques. She tapped the glass over one sepia-tinted picture. "Here's a picture of the big boulder in the creek at Hughes Park, across from Church Street. Have you been there yet?"

"It looks the same, but it's in color now instead of all brown." Nora squinted.

"The brown is just the way photos were in the old days. Anyway, the boulder makes the creek jut around it in a V-shape, which gives our creek its name. And this picture here is the Raven Mine, where one of the largest gold nuggets was ever found in the state. Here are a few tools people used to mine gold."

"This finds gold?" Logan pointed to a tiny pair of pliers.

"Oops, no. Those were used by the dentist way back then to extract teeth." She'd put them on a different shelf than the gold-mining stuff, but the placard describing the dentistry tools had slipped. She had too many items and not enough space for them all.

Nora squealed and cupped her cheeks as if to protect them from the implement. Logan's eyes lit up as he looked at his dad as if for approval.

"And this photo here, the fellow with the big mustache? That's Sheriff Fleetwood. He's the stuff of legend." As well as Faith's second cousin a few times removed.

"Did he—?" Logan glanced at her, then clamped his lips shut.

She met Logan's gaze, the sweet dark depths full of curiosity and hesitation. His shyness touched her in that part of herself that was still a shy kid herself, so she grinned. "Did he what? Catch bad guys?"

Logan nodded.

"He sure did. There are lots of books about him, including one for kids your age written by a local author. I have a stack of them on the shelf right by the cash register. See them over there? You can go get a copy and take it home with you. A gift from me."

"Where are your manners, guys?" Tom called after the kids, who'd taken off running to the cash register.

Both kids spun around. "Thanks!" Nora's gratitude echoed off the walls.

"Thank you." Logan's voice was softer, but he was smiling.

"You're welcome."

Tom looked surprised. "I'd be happy to buy it."

"It's my little way of welcoming them to town. It's got to be a big change for them, moving here."

"It is, but they're excited, too. New house, new school, more time with their grandparents."

"I'm glad." Loss and change could be devastating to a child. Or an adult. But that was not a conversation she wanted to have with a near stranger. Especially when she was trying to talk him out of pursuing occupancy in the building next door.

She tapped her fingernail against the cabinet, redirecting his attention back to the previous topic of conversation. "This stuff here is just a fraction of what I've gathered. I have items from each of the original twenty shops here on Main Street—the dentist, the post office, the assayer, the barber, all of them. Plus, documents and artifacts from the Native people groups, as well as the mines, especially the Raven. The people of this town and tourists should have the opportunity to be enriched by learning about what happened here. We shouldn't lose our ties to our past. And if the city council can't fund it, I will. I have the items and the knowledge to guide visitors through the museum. Surely, you can see the merits of my plan."

"I'm all for education, and yes, museums are important." Tom's gaze left hers as Roscoe tugged on the leash, clearly wanting to explore an Edwardian sofa. Tom's grin was sheepish. "I appreciate you letting me bring Roscoe inside. I would've normally left him at home, but there are contracting crews coming in and out today."

She would've liked to keep talking about the museum in hopes of persuading him to let her have the building, but he'd turned the conversation. Oh, well. She was trusting God with it, right? "Where's your house?"

"At the end of Arroyo Road. The house used to belong to the Miller family."

She knew the place, a mid-century modern with a glass wall offering a view of the creek behind it. "I'm sure your parents are delighted to have you and the kids back in town."

His smile shifted, no longer reaching his eyes. "They are. We stayed with them for a week, until we could move into the house. Still a few things to do, though. I'm looking forward to getting settled—not just the house, but the business."

Thanks, God, for him returning the conversation back to the building. "An outdoor gear store, you said?"

"There isn't one within twenty-five miles, which is too bad, because of our proximity to excellent camping spots, bike paths and hiking trails. That old livery is a fantastic location for one. I'm going to push out the back wall where the office is to accommodate a putting green, mount a rock climbing wall on the stone wall for—"

"A what?"

"Putting green?"

"No. A rock wall, you said?"

"You know, so people who want to try rock climbing can practice in a safe environment. A wholesome activity for kids, too. They're popular."

Oh, she knew. She'd tried one a few years ago when she visited a friend in Sacramento. But she also now knew something that would give her leverage over him when it came to the city council's decision.

The store would be hers, and all she had to do was keep her mouth shut.

But she wouldn't sleep at night if she didn't tell him the truth. Tom might be her opponent, but she wasn't the sort of person to step on someone. Not when she could help him find another way. One that didn't make them adversaries.

"Tom, the building next door isn't right for you at all. But I just thought of something even better."

Tom's stomach knotted with doubt. "What do you mean, not right for me?"

Of course, it was right for him. It was perfect.

Faith Latham, with her innocent-looking wide green eyes, was up to something.

She shrugged. "City council is pretty specific about what you can and can't do with these original buildings here on Main Street. You can't remove walls, for one thing."

Was that so? "I'm pretty sure I heard you say you were going to remove a wall so you could connect the two spaces."

"No, I'm going to reopen the sealed-off door, which is different."

Okay, maybe it was. But maybe it wasn't. "You sure about that?"

"Of course I am. I'm devoted to preserving town heritage, and while the statutes set aside for these original buildings allow for alteration to accommodate state and local codes, comfort, health and safety, they can't be remodeled. No removing walls or mounting things like a rock wall that would damage or permanently alter the walls is allowed."

Was this a lie, concocted to trick him out of applying to rent the building? If it was, it was easy enough to check the facts. One visit to the city council and he'd have his answer…which told him Faith wasn't lying.

Besides, he'd had some experience with deceitful colleagues back at the advertising agency, and Faith gave off no indications of fibbing. Her gaze didn't drift to the left. Her fingers didn't twitch. Her gaze was so steady on his, he could see the gold flecks in their green depths.

Disappointment filled his chest. "No rock wall."

"But I have a better idea for you, Tom. Seriously. *New construction.* You could have as high a rock wall as you want, and a zip line, if your insurance can handle it. Closer to the highway, there's plenty of room for a huge store like that. Plus, you'll be both visible and accessible to tourists on their way farther up into the Sierra Nevada."

He'd already considered that idea and nixed it. "If I built by the freeway, tourists wouldn't come into Widow's Peak Creek proper, though. I'd prefer those types of tourists to come *into* town and support the businesses here on Main Street. That's my way of investing in the town."

"I see your point, I do, but—you can't knock out a wall or drill into the existing stonework. So as much as I appreciate your intention to draw business here, it won't work."

Then he'd have to get around it, because this was the best location for him. The *only* location. "If I can't have a rock wall, fine, but I want my store here for two reasons, and they're sitting right over there." He looked at his kids, who'd plopped against the shop counter to peruse the book Faith had told them about. Nora read the simple text aloud to Logan, who hadn't quite caught up to her when it came to literacy skills.

Faith glanced at the kids, then met his gaze. "I'm not sure I understand."

"My wife died last year."

"I'd heard about your loss. I'm so sorry."

"Thank you." His voice came out half-strangled.

Would he ever be able to get through this without coming unglued? He took a deep, steadying breath.

"My parents live right behind Main Street, an easy walk for the kids once they're older. That's not possible if my store is located somewhere else. The store must be close to school, family, and home. I won't fail my kids by being unavailable or missing out on their lives ever again."

He caught the narrowing of her eyes when he said the word *fail*. But it was true. He'd utterly failed them. And his wife. She may have been an equal partner in their lifestyle choice—which included him working all the time—but she was gone now, and everything had changed. Tom could no longer work sixty-to-eighty-hour weeks. Nor did he want to. That old way of doing things didn't work anymore, which is what had drawn him to church in the first place.

Then everything had changed.

He still kicked himself over how little he'd been around when Lourdes was alive, and his parents helped drive the topic home, too. He couldn't change the past, but he could change the present and the future, which is why he'd moved them to the stable environment of Widow's Peak Creek. Opening a store right here on Main Street was a crucial part of that new beginning.

"This is all about my kids." Surely, Faith could understand that.

"I appreciate your intention to be an available father, Tom." The way Faith's eyes dulled, it was obvious she'd been hurt by something in her past. "And son."

He almost laughed at that last part. His parents didn't trust him a lick because he'd been an unavailable dad. No wonder they'd made him promise to do everything he could to put the kids first, forsaking all distractions, from hobbies to dating.

As if he'd be interested in dating again. Ha.

A thud on the floor tugged their gazes to the front counter. The kids stood, shoulders tense, beside a fallen umbrella stand. Logan seemed frozen, eyes wide.

"Sorry," Nora said.

"It's all right." Faith's smile looked real, as if it hadn't bothered her in the slightest.

Tom rushed to set the umbrella stand to rights. "We've taken up enough of your time. I'll let you open your store now."

She laughed. "Thanks, but first I'd better submit my application to rent the old livery."

He'd really hoped she'd hear his story and decide his need for the old livery was greater than her desire for a museum in the space. It seemed they'd be duking it out at city council, though. "I'd better get moving on my application, too." And start praying.

"Goodbye, Tom." The hand she extended for shaking was soft and small in his hand.

She really was a nice person, with a well-intentioned plan for the community. But one of them would be disappointed when it came to renting the storefront next door.

And as nice as she was, Tom had no intention of losing the building to her.

Chapter Three

At a few minutes before ten o'clock the next morning, the cloudless sky's soft blue hue matched the bicycle in Faith's display window. She paused to admire the glorious spring day when she propped the shop door ajar, allowing the gentle breeze to ruffle her hair and her red print midi skirt patterned with teacups. She inhaled deeply the smells of fresh cut grass and sharp flowering pear tree blossoms. Her seasonal allergies might make her regret it, but she couldn't resist relishing in the promise of a spring morning.

You make all things new, Lord. Even my spirits after suffering some disappointments yesterday with the mayor and Tom Santos.

Maybe things could be new with her family, too. Or at least *better*. Something about Tom's manner yesterday made her think things weren't all peaches and cream in his relationship with his parents, but they were helping him with his kids and clearly supporting him in his time of need. It made Faith yearn for familial connection, too. Her parents and sister were alive and well, but it had been so long since she'd seen them, much less talked to them.

The strain she felt with her family wasn't entirely her fault, but she bore her share of the blame. The way they prioritized the newest material things, she'd always felt as if she'd been born into the wrong family, sticking out like an antimacassar-draped vintage chair placed in a showroom among sleek, modern furniture.

Her family loved her, though, just as she loved them. Should she reach out?

Not right now to her mother, who was in Hawaii with her husband, Gary. Nor her father, who was on a business trip in Europe with his wife, Valerie.

What about her sister, Chloe? Her job in San Francisco wasn't the sort that had her on the road much. She should be available. She might not understand Faith's devotion to antiques, but she could provide a little support anyway, couldn't she?

Before she could talk herself out of it, Faith found Chloe's contact in her phone and pressed the call button.

She should've expected Chloe's voice mail—Chloe was working, after all—but her stomach still felt hollow when her sister didn't pick up.

At the beep, Faith smiled so her voice would sound peppy, a trick she'd learned in a magazine. "Hi, Chloe, long time no talk. I hope you're well, and uh…" She was so not good at this type of thing. "I just wanted to talk. I'm fine. Honest. But do you remember me telling you about my idea at Christmastime, to open a museum next door to the shop? Funny story, that's not funny at all, but someone else wants the building to open an outdoor gear store. Tom Santos. I'm sure you remember him from high school. Anyway, now I've got to compete against him for the space at a city council meeting in twelve days and I'm nervous. I have to make up a presentation, and I—"

The phone beeped. The mailbox must be full or something. Sighing, Faith ended the call.

After hanging the open sign on the front door, she carried her sandwich chalkboard outside to welcome customers. She situated the sign, filled the doggy water dish for any canine visitors and dusted the green chairs set outside her door. Today, she topped the tiny café table between the seats with three straw baskets filled with odds and ends and a small chalkboard sign reading *$1*.

"Hey!" a feminine voice called.

Looking up, Faith grinned at her assistant, who was wearing a dressy black top tucked into white skinny jeans. Angie Chang was more than Faith's employee. She'd become Faith's closest friend, and today she had a white bag from Angel Food Bakery in her hand.

Faith's stomach pinched with hunger. "Are those raspberry almond scones?"

Gently, Angie shook the bag. "After the day you had yesterday, I thought you could use a treat."

Angie had come into work yesterday right after Tom and his kids left, and Faith had given her a full recap. By the way Angie was clenching her jaw this morning, she was still as upset about the situation as Faith was. "I'm so mad at the mayor I could—well, aren't we supposed to keep our mouths shut if we can't say anything nice?"

"Good advice." Faith followed her inside the store. "But thank you." She hugged her friend, scone bag between them, grateful. She couldn't count on her family's support, but she had Angie's, and that was no small thing.

When Angie pulled away, she shook the bag again. "Let's focus our attention on the scones."

Faith poured them both cups of fresh-brewed tea—today's blend was English breakfast—and bit into the treat. The sweet-tart taste of raspberries filled her mouth.

Delicious. Dabbing her lips with a paper napkin, she gave Angie a thumbs-up. "Thanks, Ange. You don't know how much I needed that."

"The scones are as much to lift my spirits as they are yours." Angie pulled her shoulder-length black hair back into a ponytail, securing it with the black elastic she'd been wearing as a bracelet. "Do you need any help working up the proposal for city council?"

"Thanks, but I don't think so. I mocked up a draft and confirmed with Maeve that the time limit allotted on each presentation is ten minutes." Maeve McInnis ran In Stitches, the yarn store four doors down, and her husband was a member of the council. "I have over a week to refine and rehearse my speech."

"I remember Tomás Santos from school." Angie took a long pull of her tea. "He was a year ahead of me. Nice guy, from what I recall."

"He's still nice." And nice-looking, too, but he could be nice a hundred ways and Faith wouldn't lose sight of the fact that he was her competitor.

"It's the mayor I'm mad at," Angie clarified.

"Things would be easier if she'd agree to allocate funds for a museum. But she won't, so here we are, trying to get a museum and keep Faith's Finds firmly in the black." The months between Christmas and Memorial Day were typically slow for her, and this year had proven to be no exception. She had to trust God to provide, yes, but she also needed to do her part and focus on selling inventory. "Do you think I should move these bracelets to the dollar basket outside?"

Angie peered at the beaded pieces dangling from the brass jewelry tree by the register. "Can you let them go for a buck?"

"They're not vintage. Just ones I made."

"They cost more than a dollar to produce, though. And they're adorable. I say give them more time." Her gaze caught on something behind Faith in the direction of the open door. "Oh, hello."

Customers? Faith spun.

Not quite customers. Two little dark-haired visitors, one wearing an orange T-shirt with blue stripes and one in a pink skirt carrying a plush unicorn. Cuties.

"Good morning, Logan, Nora."

"We drew you a picture." Nora rushed to hand her a folded piece of yellow construction paper.

It read, *Thank you for the book* in childish block script, surrounded by crayon flowers, a car, a yellow dog, a gray cat and a—hmm. Faith wasn't sure what that blob was. The kids had also signed their names in all capital letters.

"I love this. Thank you. Hey, meet my friend Angie." She turned to Angie. "These are Tom Santos's kids."

"You told her about us?" Nora tipped her head like a bird. Logan, however, kept quiet like yesterday, eyeing the checkerboard on the farmhouse table.

"Of course," Angie said. "Welcome to town."

"Welcome to you, too." Nora curtsied. "Where's Bet-teeny?"

"Bettina?" Faith bit back a smile. "She's upstairs, napping."

"Her name should be Bet-teeny because she's *so little*." On the last two words, Nora's voice was higher pitched than a cartoon mouse's.

Logan side-eyed the checkerboard again. "We can see Bet-teeny later, Nora. We gotta hurry."

At that suspicious statement, Faith folded her arms. "Where's your dad?"

"Next door." Nora pulled Logan over to the checkerboard. "We came to give you the paper and visit Bet-teeny and play checkers."

Surely, he'd been the one to send them over with the paper, but Faith exchanged a glance with Angie. "He knows you're here, right? Delivering the card."

Logan pulled the red checkers toward him. "I'm red, Nora."

That wasn't an answer. "Does your dad know where you are right now?"

"Nora! Logan!" Tom's frantic tones carried in from outside. That answered that question.

Faith rushed to the door and stuck her head outside. Tom stood outside the wide-open door of the old livery, frantically searching the street, chest heaving beneath his plaid flannel shirt from obvious panic. Much as she didn't like that he'd been inside the vacant building, his panic was far more pressing. "Tom, they're here."

His hand went to his heart as he met her gaze. Poor man. He brushed past her into the store and shook his head as he made a beeline for his kids. "You two about scared me out of my skin. What are you doing here?"

"We brought Miss Faith her card." Nora pulled her unicorn over her face.

"I said I'd bring you here when we were finished."

"It was boring in the old liver-house." Logan moved a checker piece.

"Livery." Tom glanced at Faith, his eyes creased around the edges with guilt.

She moved closer to him so she could lower her voice. "They brought me a card so I assumed you'd sent them over, but I was asking them about it when I heard you call out." It was important to her that he knew she was a responsible adult, even if they were in competition with one another.

"They can be crafty—and I don't mean arts and crafts–type crafty. They're quick." He stepped back to the door like he was leaving, but instead he waved at someone down the street and then gave a thumbs-up.

A man around Faith's age jogged past the display window, into the store. His blond hair and prominent cheekbones weren't the least bit familiar. "Thank God, Tom."

"They came in here to deliver a note." Tom rolled his eyes and then gestured to Faith. "Ender Strong, Faith Latham. He used to work in a camping gear store so I'm picking his brain. Ender, meet Faith Latham and—" He smiled at Angie. "Your name is Angela, right?"

"Angie Chang." She flipped her ponytail over her shoulder and darted glances at Ender. *Huh.*

"Anyway." Tom rounded on the kids. "You left without asking permission. I had no idea where you were. You know better than that."

Nora rushed to embrace his legs. "Sorry, Daddy."

"Me, too." Logan stepped close enough for Tom to touch on the head.

He whispered something to the kids, then offered Faith a small smile. "Sorry. They must have distracted you from your work."

"It's no problem." Faith liked children. Always assumed she'd have some, but she was nearly thirty and her one big relationship had been a disaster on par with the Titanic sinking. Would she ever have her own kids? Not in the foreseeable future. But she could hang out with other people's kids to get a fix, right? "They can stay and play checkers if they want."

Logan jumped up and down. "Can we, Daddy?"

"If you're sure." Tom's eyes were on Faith.

"Honest. I don't mind." They didn't have any customers, anyway.

"Just one game." Tom nodded at the kids and they rushed to the checkerboard.

Out of the corner of her eye, she saw Ender approach Angie and they moved to the tea cart. Faith expected Tom to return to the *old liver-house*, but he moved toward her instead, rubbing the back of his neck.

She might as well ask the uncomfortable question she'd been mulling since the kids arrived. "What are you doing next door, if you don't mind my asking?"

"Mayor Hughes loaned me the key so I can draw up plans for my proposal."

Oh, she had, had she? Granted, there was nothing unfair or wrong about the mayor allowing Tom inside the livery, but it would have been nice to have been afforded the same opportunity. "I'll have to ask her the same favor, then." She kept her tone calm and conversational, fully deserving of an Academy Award, considering the way irritation pricked at her stomach.

He rubbed his jaw, drawing her attention to the appealing dark stubble on his cheeks and chin. Well, that chased her irritation away, and her stomach filled with whooshing butterflies.

She looked away, fast.

It wasn't enough, though. He twisted a half step toward her, close enough to envelop her in the radius of his citrusy cologne. She hadn't noticed the scent yesterday, which was a good thing, because the butterflies in her belly went ballistic, spreading to her limbs and messing up whatever thought she'd entertained five seconds ago. Tom smelled good. So good she wanted to step closer and take a deep sniff of his flannel shirt and—

Whoa. She'd never reacted to cologne like this before. Or stubble, which, if she were honest, suited him. It looked less like he was growing a beard and more like he was a Hollywood star making a fashion statement. He was a nice-looking man, but no, no, a thousand times no—she was not going to think about him like *that*. Like he was romance material.

She regained a fraction of her sanity when she took a step back on the pretense of reaching for the dust rag behind the counter and buffing the already-clean space, gulping the less interesting wood polish smell of her shop.

"So." She scrambled for a sane thing to say. "How are the kids adjusting?"

"They start school tomorrow," Tom half whispered, which explained why he'd stepped so close to her. "It might sound odd to start a new school on a Friday, but the teacher and I decided this might help them ease back into things. Anyway, they're nervous, so I thought I'd take them out, get their minds off school tomorrow. I'm sorry for the interruption."

"We weren't busy." Thankfully, her voice sounded normal. Her pulse was still fast, though. *Talk about something normal.* "I don't remember your friend from school."

"He didn't attend WPC High. His grandma is my parents' next-door neighbor, and he visited every July."

"Ah, a summer kid, just like me."

"But you went to WPC High, didn't you? We talked about it yesterday, and I remember—well, I remember Chloe."

Of course he did—everyone remembered Chloe. "My sister graduated here, but she's two years older than I am. Our parents divorced that year and we all moved to San Francisco. I came back here to visit my grandparents during the summers, though, and when I was self-sufficient, I moved here." Where she'd been the happiest. "Does Ender live here now, too, or is he visiting you?"

"He lives here now and works at the auto-parts store, but he has experience with camping goods, so he's my first hire." Tom's expression grew wistful. "And he's a good friend. Since my wife's funeral, he's been like a brother to me."

Tom was an only child, unlike Faith, who just felt like one sometimes. Hopefully, Chloe would get back to her this time, though. "I'm glad he was there for you."

He looked over at Ender and Angie chatting over their cups of tea. "My wife's death was sudden, and since then I've struggled with worrying about the twins. When they disappeared just now, I about lost it."

Faith's heart ached in her chest. "That's totally understandable. You're a caring dad."

"My goal is to be a better dad each day."

"It's obvious how much you love them, and you'd never let anything happen to them, Tom."

"Thanks for saying that, Faith. Sometimes I feel like the worst parent in the world. I—"

A loud crash outside, followed by breaking glass, made Faith jump. "Oh, no."

She hurried out front, where the green chairs lay on their sides and the contents of her dollar baskets spilled over the sidewalk. The mason jar she'd filled with dried flowers had shattered into pieces, and books lay on the dirty ground. Decorative drawer knobs rolled into the street.

And Nora and Logan were in the middle of the mess, crying, definitely not playing checkers inside. Their dad had said they were crafty, but Faith hadn't understood just how fast, or quiet, they were. How had she missed them slinking out of the store?

It didn't matter right now, the way they were crying. Faith started to reach for them, but Tom took them in hand, gathering them to his sides. "Are you hurt?"

Nora repeated something, muffled by the unicorn pressed against her face. *Sorry*, that's what it was. Logan shook his head. A quick scan assured Faith both kids were unharmed, just scared. They would be fine, and they were with their dad, where they belonged.

Faith stepped back to set the chairs right side up so the group approaching on the sidewalk wouldn't trip on them. Oh—they weren't tourists. They were local boys out of high school, a surly set, and she wasn't surprised when one of them trod over the already-shattered jar.

"Stupid old junk."

Shame burned hot in her chest. She had nothing to be ashamed of, but *stupid old junk* was a sentiment she'd heard before. Not in those words, exactly, but her parents, sister and folks like Mayor Hughes all looked down on Faith's Finds.

And when others viewed the precious items in her store as nothing but old junk, well, it wasn't anything she hadn't heard before from the people who were supposed to love her the most.

Holding his kids close, Tom swallowed down remorse. Anger, too. His kids had escaped his notice twice in ten minutes. What kind of father was he?

One who was trying to do better, that's what kind.

That meant he needed to watch them like a proverbial hawk but also ensure they respected the rules. Now that their tears were subsiding, he loosened his hold a fraction. "So what happened, guys?"

"We fell off the chairs." Nora wiped her tears on his shirt.

"Like this." Logan made a crash sound.

"So you climbed on chairs that are meant for sitting on. And collided with the table, looks like."

Nora sniffled into his stomach. "It was an ask-ident."

Faith looked up from gathering stuff off the sidewalk. "Of course it was, and I'm just glad you're not hurt."

Her tone was far sweeter than Tom's might have been

had his display been demolished. She'd set the green chairs upright, but knickknacks were still scattered over the concrete sidewalk and jewel-toned items had rolled into the asphalt street.

Tom started to let go of his kids for the items, but Faith dashed into the street. In a few moments, she'd retrieved the items and dumped them—drawer knobs—into one of the baskets.

Sorry, he mouthed at her.

She waved off his silent apology.

She shouldn't have to clean the mess, though. "Guys, help Miss Faith pick up the things you knocked down. Watch the glass there, though."

"I'll get a dustpan," Angie said behind him. He hadn't even realized she was out here.

The twins crouched to scoop up the oversized buttons, thimbles and pins that had spilled, dropping them into the baskets. Faith smiled as she repositioned the baskets on the table. "Thanks for the help."

Tom took the dustpan from Angie. Glass shards tinkled as Tom brushed up the broken glass, along with a few dry leaves. "Guys, didn't we just have a talk, like, two minutes ago, about you not going places without telling me?"

"We didn't go anywhere," Logan protested.

"You left the store."

"We were just at the door," Nora said. "We wanted to see what was in the baskets."

"Standing by the door isn't leaving," Logan added.

Six years old and his children were masters of semantics. Tom took a deep breath. "You went outside without permission. That counts as leaving, and I'm pretty sure you two know it. I'm just sorry I didn't see you do it."

Nora jogged on her tippy-toes, bent over. "That's because we ran like this when you were looking at Ender and the other lady."

Bad enough that he hadn't noticed his kids leaving the store, but now that he knew they'd deliberately snuck past him when he was looking in the other direction, he had another lesson to impart to them. One he hoped to do well, so he prayed before he spoke.

"You two are the most important things in the world to me, which is why I can't allow you to break our family rules. You know that means consequences. First, you both owe Miss Faith an apology for wrecking her display."

"Sorry." Nora stopped moving for a half second to apologize.

"Sorry." Logan wasn't as penitent sounding as Tom would've liked, but they'd have a talk about that later.

"Thank you." Faith offered each of his kids fist bumps. "I'm just glad you didn't get hurt."

Tom hoped his gratitude shone in his eyes well enough for her to recognize it. She smiled, so it seemed like she did. Hopefully, she wouldn't mind what he was about to do next.

"Miss Faith can't sell some of this merchandise now. It's broken. We need to pay for it."

Faith shook her head. "It's just an old jar I used as a vase."

"The knobs are dinged up. I'm sure other things got dirty, at least. We owe you for that."

"Truly, this stuff isn't valuable. That's why it's outside."

"I want my kids to learn actions have consequences, though, and they broke a big rule today. Twice. They can do extra chores at home and they can *pay* you what they earn, or if it isn't too much trouble, they could do a chore for you after school or on the weekend. I'll stick around to supervise, of course. What sounds better to you?"

She bit her lower lip. Maybe she disagreed with his parenting techniques. Well, he was new at this, despite being a dad for six years. Lourdes had made and enforced the rules, but everything was different now.

"They can come here Saturday afternoon," Faith said at last. "I have a few jars of change that need sorting."

Logan smiled. "I like money."

"You don't get to keep it," Tom reminded him. Once he and Faith settled the details of the kids' working for her, he tipped his head at his kids. "Now we should probably get out of Miss Faith's way."

"What about our checker game?" Nora's little lips pouted.

"I'll keep an eye on them, Tom," Ender offered.

"Okay." He wanted another minute to talk to Faith, anyway. When the others returned inside, he shoved his hands into his jeans pockets. "I'm really sorry."

"Thanks, but it's all right. What sort of antiques store owner would I be if I didn't have a mess every so often?"

"Thanks for being so good with my kids."

"I like them. We'll have fun sorting coins." She grinned. "Maybe I should show them a photograph of what your great-grandfather contributed to the town."

"What do you mean? You know about my family?"

"It's public record, part of town history, so yeah. See the stone foundation there?"

At first, he thought she was pointing to the door alongside her shop window, which undoubtedly led to an upstairs apartment. Then he realized she meant the health-food store next door, separated from Faith's Finds by a narrow alley, where a foot or so of river rock formed the building's foundation below wood siding that had been painted McIntosh-apple red. "At Apple a Day?"

"Your great-grandfather did that work. He was a mason."

"No kidding?"

"He came here during the gold rush to make his fortune but found it didn't pay as well as masonry. You didn't know that?"

He shook his head. "I wonder if my father knows. I'll ask him later."

On their way back inside the store, she adjusted a sandwich chalkboard on which she'd written the name of the store and a handful of words:

Old, Vintage, Antique, Loved.

Something about the way she tweaked it, looked at it with a critical eye and then smiled, hit him hot in the solar plexus. This was about love for her. She was a person of care and kindness, with her store, this town, even his kids.

That made her even prettier in his eyes, and she was already stunning, her soft wavy hair a perfect complement to her green-flecked eyes.

Wait, what? No. He was not going there. He could objectively find her pretty, although he hadn't thought about a woman that way since Lourdes. But anything more than that?

Nope. He was all about the future, for him and his kids. And that did not include being attracted to Faith Latham.

Chapter Four

A gentle but steady rain fell Saturday afternoon, and lit by cut glass lamps, the antiques store had a cozy, homey feel. Not too many customers dropped in on rainy days like this, so Faith used the lull to dust the tea sets and dishes—always one of her biggest sellers. The work was repetitive but mindless, enabling her to think and pray about her proposal for the museum.

It was a pity Mayor Hughes didn't want a decent museum here, considering her ties to the town's history. The park by the creek where the water flowed around a massive boulder, giving it its "widow's peak" shape, was named after an ancestor of the mayor's husband, after all. But the mayor's mind was clearly not on Aesop Hughes's discovery of a massive nugget nearby in 1851. It was on tax dollars, and Tom's store would provide tax revenue, for sure.

But it would do the same somewhere else in town, though. It didn't need to be next door.

At least Angie supported her, as well as a few friends like Maeve down the street. It would be nice to add Chloe to that list, but her sister hadn't yet returned her call. Maybe she hadn't received it?

Or, more likely, other things were more important to Chloe. Faith shouldn't have expected more but it still ached deep down.

Westminster Chimes dinged out from the grandfather clock, striking one o'clock the moment the store door opened. Tom and the twins, donned in damp rain jackets, stood on the rug, stomping water from their boots. "Hello, there."

"Hi, Miss Faith." Nora shoved back her hood, revealing her hair fixed up in a tidy French braid. "Like my hair?"

"Oh, yes."

Tom raked his hair back away from his brow, mussing it in an endearing way. "My mom did it. I tried first, though."

Now that was more endearing than his mussy hair. "Did you?"

Nora rolled her eyes. "Daddy's terrible at it."

Logan looked up at Faith, his dark eyes wide and serious. "Where's Bet-teeny?"

He was so cute—both kids were cute in their own way, and Faith's heart swelled with burgeoning affection for both of them. Nora never stood still and seemed to have no fear. Logan, however, was uncertain about things and clingier with his dad. Maybe he'd struggled since losing his mom.

Faith tapped his nose. "Resting somewhere. I'm sure she'll wake up while we're sorting coins today."

Nora looked around the store. "Where's your friend?"

"Miss Angie? On a date at the train museum in Sacramento with your daddy's friend Ender." She glanced at Tom. Had he known their friends got along like chips and guacamole? Before he could say anything, though, the phone rang. "Excuse me a sec."

"Take your time." Tom shrugged out of his olive green jacket.

"Faith's Finds," she said into the receiver, as she gathered her pen and notepad. "How may I help you?"

"Hi, Faith, it's Willa Carew at the Cordova Inn," said the familiar voice. "We love the buffet you found so much that I'm hoping you have another unique piece for the inn's parlor."

Yay and yay—two pieces of good news. "That's great to hear, and yes, absolutely. Are you thinking of filling that area by the window?"

"How'd you guess?" Willa chuckled. "I want something outside the box."

Nora took a step onto the red-carpeted staircase that led to Faith's apartment, ducking under the gold cord Faith used to discourage customers from trekking upstairs. "I found Bet-teeny!"

Sure enough, Bettina was curled up on the landing four steps up. Tom smiled at Faith and then made a shushing sound. "Miss Faith is on the phone," he whispered. "Let's take your damp jackets off before they make a mess."

Faith jotted notes while Willa listed her ideas, but her gaze kept darting to Tom as he hung their outerwear on the tree rack by the front door. He caught her looking and she stared down at the notepad. "I have a rosewood game table, early nineteenth century, claw feet, with a folding top that reveals an inlaid chessboard. Does that sound interesting enough?"

"Text me pictures, but it sounds perfect," Willa said

into her ear. "You have great taste and you know what kind of vibe we're going for here at the Cordova."

The boutique hotel in Sacramento was an eclectic blend of vintage and modern, which created a fun yet restful atmosphere in Faith's opinion. "I'll send you the measurements, too."

"If you have anything else interesting and different, let me know. We'll be refurbishing some rooms next month, and much as I love antiques, our customers have told us they also appreciate contemporary touches to accommodate technology. My grandma's old secretary desk is adorable, but I can barely fit my laptop on it."

"Oh, I understand. A lot of pieces were smaller back when. Designed for different needs."

After a few more details, Faith ended the call and strode toward the little group sitting on the stairs to her apartment, patting her cat. "Sorry about that."

"Nothing to apologize for. Sounds like you made a sale."

"Possibly, yeah. I helped the Cordova Inn in Sacramento with an antique buffet for their breakfast room, and though their furnishings are a diverse mix in styles, it's nice they kept me in mind this time, too. I'll send over photos of the game table there."

"It's gorgeous. I wonder how long it took to make something like that." He ambled toward the square table in question, tracing his lean finger over the hand-carved rim.

Nice to see he admired quality workmanship. "It's over a hundred and fifty years old. Just imagine what sorts of conversations were held at this table over the decades while families or young couples played games on it by candlelight."

He looked at her as if he'd come to a realization. "It's not just about the age and value of a thing for you, is it? It's the story."

"The story, the legacy, yes. Whether it's the heritage of an object, or a town, they're both important."

Tom's face grew serious. "About that. The kids and I visited the bookstore this morning. We met the manager. Kellan?"

"Sure. Did the kids join the book club? Buy ten children's books, get one free?"

"Yeah." Tom scratched his stubbly chin. "Kellan was telling me he's an avid mountain biker."

She'd seen him biking, but that wasn't uncommon around here. "This is a good place for him to live, then."

"And Gwen at Apple a Day? She gets her kayak gear online, and said she'd be glad for the ability to browse a sporting goods store on her lunch breaks. Claudia at Angel Food says her husband fishes a lot and the folks at Del's Café think if there's a new store on the block, more tourists will visit for lunch. Same with the restaurant, Emerald's—"

"Wait a second." Her hand rose to stop him. "You've been talking to the other Main Street shopkeepers about your store to, what, get them on your side?"

"I was gauging the desire of local folks for a store like mine, but their enthusiasm confirmed my suspicions. My store will do well anywhere in town, but next door, it will flourish."

These other shopkeepers weren't just her fellow business folk on Main Street. She'd counted them—Kellan, Gwen, Claudia, George and Sandy, all of them—as friends, but they preferred his idea over hers? Twin sensations of rejection and betrayal twisted hot and liquid in her core. "I can't believe it."

"That they're interested in my store?"

"No, that you talked to them like that." She stomped to the farthest corner of the store, adjusting bowls that didn't need adjusting.

Tom hurried after her. "It's not unethical, Faith. I wasn't asking for their support, just their opinions."

"Which I'm sure you'll mention in your city council proposal."

"You'd do the same."

He had a point, but until this moment, she hadn't realized the other shopkeepers—at least the ones Tom had mentioned—preferred his plan for the vacant building. Even though it was business, it felt personal.

Swallowing down the unpleasant emotions in her throat, she lifted her head. "I'm not giving up, Tom."

"No one wants you to give up a museum, but I had a fantastic idea when the kids and I walked to the park the other day—Logan was hoping to climb the big boulder and roll his cars off it, but of course that was a big no. Anyway, we passed the old schoolhouse, and it's just sitting there, vacant, turning into an eyesore. Why don't you put your museum there?"

Her stomach soured like she'd chugged buttermilk. "Are you serious?"

"It's small, but it doesn't sound like you need a lot of room, based on what I've seen." He gestured at her lone cabinet of photos and artifacts. "A paint job and new windows, and that place will be good as new. It's centrally located—"

"And in terrible shape. It's the third schoolhouse they built here, not original, so the town hasn't done anything to preserve it, not like they have the little church. No insulation, no electricity for a security system, much less lights. And it is indeed small. Too small. I couldn't display half of what I have in there."

He snapped his fingers, clearly undeterred. "So you rotate stock. Since it's not original to the town, we can give it a total refurbishment, maybe even add on to the footprint. I worked in marketing so I can help you make a great-looking presentation for city council."

Great. He had experience making professional pitches. Now she knew when it came to their city council presentations, her simple PowerPoint would be a lot less flashy than whatever he did to showcase his idea. Antique David up against tech-savvy Goliath.

No matter what happened, though, she had no intention of occupying the one-room schoolhouse. "I'd love to fix it up, but it won't matter what we do because I'm not putting a museum in there. Like I mentioned to you on Day One, I need to be able to run the store and the museum at the same time. I can't do that if the museum is at the end of the block."

"Unless you hire help."

"I'm not in a position to do that right now." Not that it was any of his business, but having another employee beyond Angie on the payroll, even for a few hours a day, was out of her budget. Besides, who would she hire who knew the artifacts and stories of the town as well as she did?

His enthusiasm morphed into something akin to concern. "Is it money? Because I'd be happy to make a donation for refurbishments. How much do you think you need?"

First, he'd talked to half the shopkeepers on the street

about their situation, and now he was offering money? He might not be bulldozing her, but she definitely felt pushed. Maybe he thought he was fixing the problem, but he was fixing it for him, not her.

She'd kept her calm, despite a storm cloud of feelings forming in her gut. Now that he'd started offering her money, though, that cloud had developed a big ol' thunderhead, and it was impossible to keep her mouth shut.

"If this were a movie, you'd be pulling out a checkbook and offering me cash to fade away."

His smile fell. "That's not what I'm doing."

"Maybe that's an exaggeration, but you're offering a solution I never asked for."

"I'm trying to help, that's all."

"*Help* me go away so you can have the old livery. But get this straight, Tom. No amount of money *in a donation* will make me change my mind." She made air quotes.

"You make it sound like a bribe." His tone tensed to match hers.

"It could be interpreted as a bribe. You pay for the renovations if I cede the store to you."

"I was trying to offer a solution." His hands clenched into fists. "But since we're on the topic of money, maybe you should think about how much cash flow it takes to run two businesses. If you don't have enough capital to pay additional employees to staff the museum, two storefronts might be more than you can handle, anyway."

He did *not* just say that.

"You're saying I can't pay my bills. Because I mentioned this is a slower season, right? How dare you."

"I'm not saying anything, just offering some advice for you to consider before you bite off more than you can chew." His hands rose in the air. "I was trying to be nice."

"Taking a building out from under me isn't what I'd call nice."

The hair on Faith's arms lifted and her gaze was drawn by the invisible tether of someone looking at her. Logan and Nora had left the cat and were staring at them with wide eyes.

Nora's little face crumpled. "You're not being nice, Daddy?"

Uh-oh.

Tom's stomach sank down to his soles. He never should have let the conversation get out of control like this. Not in front of his kids, not at all. But she'd accused him of throwing money at her museum when he was trying to find a solution for both of them. All he had to show for his gesture was high blood pressure and his pulse pounding in his ears.

And two little kids staring at him like he'd broken the golden rule. "Umm—"

"Of course, he's a nice man. We're just having a grown-up conversation." Faith's smile was obviously fake, but he was grateful for her effort. Clearly, she was as upset as he was, judging by her trembling hands. She clasped them together, probably so his kids wouldn't see.

Logan narrowed his eyes. "Daddy has his frowny face on."

Tom knew better than to tell his kids not to trust their own eyes, but he had to offer some sort of explanation to smooth over this mess. "It's been a long day already, that's all."

"That means he's tired or crabby." Nora glanced up at Faith. "Before we came over here, Daddy and Grammy had a grown-up conversation with frowny faces, too."

Great. "That's family stuff, Nora."

Faith's smile looked genuine now. "Every family has frowny-faced conversations from time to time."

Logan's brows knit. "Yours, too?"

"Absolutely," Faith answered before Tom could put a stop to the personal line of inquiry. "Disagreements aren't bad. We just have to be careful we don't say mean things. And when we do, we say we're sorry."

"Do they say sorry, too?" Nora fingered a table edge.

"My family doesn't live in Widow's Peak Creek anymore, and you know what, I haven't seen my parents or my sister in a while. Isn't that funny?"

Her nonanswer said it all. There was some sort of hurt between her and her family. From what Tom remembered of Faith's sister, Chloe, she was all glitter and new toys. He couldn't imagine her working alongside Faith in an antiques store, much less shopping in one. Had the sisters' differences caused tension?

If so, he could relate. Things with his parents had been strained since Lourdes died, and hadn't improved much since he'd quit his job and brought the kids back to Widow's Peak Creek. What would it take to prove to them that Logan and Nora were his top priority now? That he wouldn't fail them again?

Maybe his parents didn't believe he could live up to his promise. Once he established his store next door, they'd see how committed he was to being there for his kids whenever they needed him.

He was sorry Faith would lose out on having her museum next door where it was convenient, but it couldn't be helped. The kids were more important. She'd said she had no intention of yielding. Well, he didn't, either.

Maybe they should get to business and get out of her

hair before they fought again. He cleared his throat, praying his voice would sound friendly now. "Is this still a good time for the kids to help work off the mess from the other day?"

"Sure." Faith avoided his gaze when she beckoned the kids to a display table. "This shouldn't take long. I find loose change in furniture I buy, and I stick it in this jar. I wondered if you guys could separate the coins for me and put them into smaller jars. One each for pennies, nickels, dimes and quarters."

"Yep," Logan answered, sounding eager. The kids perched on chairs at the table as she brought over a gallon-sized jar half full of coins.

Gently, Faith poured the money out onto the tabletop. The kids' eyes grew wide as they touched the spilled coins.

"Gonna help us, Daddy?" Nora glanced up.

If it would hurry this along so they could leave the store, sure thing. "Sure." He pulled a few pennies toward him. "Do we need to count them, too?"

"No, just sort." Faith dropped two pint jars on the table. "Thanks."

Tom's phone buzzed in his front jeans pocket. His mom's name was on the screen. "Hey, Mom."

"You have to come home. Right now." Her voice trembled with panic.

"What's wrong? Is Dad okay?" Dad had planned on playing tennis with a friend in Sacramento today, but they probably weren't out on the court with this rain. But what if Dad had never made it to visit his friend? Tom's stomach sank to depths he hadn't known existed until Lourdes died. Did Dad have a car accident?

"Your dad's fine. It's Roscoe. He's sick or something, and I cannot do this, Tom. I know I said he could stay here today but I have a showing in an hour and I can't leave him here, making messes."

Even though he was worried about his dog, relief pooled through Tom's gut. Seemed like every time someone called him anymore and didn't sound 100 percent calm, he automatically went to the darkest place he'd ever been, that call telling him Lourdes was gone. *Thank you that Dad's okay, Lord.*

But Roscoe didn't sound too good. "Can you describe what's wrong with him?"

"I don't know. He's throwing up."

"Sounds like he might need the vet." Tom rubbed his suddenly aching forehead. "I'll be right there."

When he turned around, three pairs of concerned eyes stared at him. Even Faith's, when two minutes ago she wouldn't look him in the eye.

He tugged his keys from his pocket. "We'd better go, kids. Roscoe's not feeling well. I'm sorry, Faith."

"No, please." She hurried to gather their coats. "I'm so sorry."

"I'm sure he'll be okay." God willing. He scrolled through his phone. "I hope there's a vet open on the weekend somewhere."

"It's on Sugar Pine Street, by the grocery store."

He knew the strip mall, nice and close. "Thanks. And kids, you have to come to the vet with me, so while I get Roscoe, grab some books at Grandma's in case there's a long wait."

Faith froze with Logan's jacket in hand. "You know what, leave the kids here."

"Can we, Daddy?" Nora clasped her hands in a begging posture. "I want to sort coins."

"Me, too." Logan slipped away from Faith, who'd been holding out his jacket.

"Are you sure?" He looked at Faith, trying to gauge her emotions. She hated his guts right now, didn't she? Accusing him of bribery—thinking about it made him mad all over again, but he had more pressing things to deal with.

She waved him off. "Just take care of Roscoe. We'll count coins and have a snack, if that's okay with you."

He hadn't left his kids with anyone except his parents in a long while. He barely knew Faith. But no matter how she felt about him, she was a decent person. His kids clearly preferred staying here to sitting in the vet lobby. "It's fine, if you're sure."

"I'm sure."

Gone were the anger and hurt he'd seen in her green eyes earlier. She might have a problem with him, but clearly, she could set it aside to care about his kids and his dog. At the realization, his anger dissolved a fraction.

Nora hugged his leg as he donned his jacket. "Tell Roscoe I love him and give him a kiss on his mouth."

"Maybe not the kiss part. He was sick."

"Ew." Logan wrinkled his nose.

"Be good for Miss Faith." Tom kissed the tops of their heads, catching whiffs of their strawberry-scented shampoo. Then he met Faith's gaze. "Thank you. Really."

"No worries."

Well, he did have worries, but he was glad someone had lessened one of them.

Except he was halfway to the vet when he realized he'd forgotten to get her cell phone number or to leave his with her. Thankfully, his kids had his number memorized, but he'd phone the store the minute he was able to just to check in.

I'm trying to do it right this time, Lord. Please help me to be the man You want me to be. Now that I know I can't do it without You, I'm counting on You.

Tom's trust had a habit of faltering at times like these. He was like a man on the edge of a frozen lake, worried if he stepped out, the ice would crack beneath his feet.

But he had no choice but to step out in faith. The dog, the kids, his parents, the store…all caused him anxiety right now. But he had to trust God was doing something here.

Even if his old self thought he was crazy.

Chapter Five

Faith set down the shop phone and turned back to the kids. "It was your dad leaving me his cell phone number and telling me Roscoe is all signed in at the vet clinic. He wanted to know how you were doing, too."

"We heard you tell him we're busy," Nora said.

Faith resumed her seat, reaching for a palm full of coins. "Your daddy thinks Roscoe ate something he shouldn't have and will be all right."

"I wonder what he got into at Grammy's." Nora stacked her pennies high rather than putting them into the penny jar.

"He's at your grandparents' house?" That explained why Tom's mom had called with the news, although the situation was curious.

Logan nodded. "There's a man working on pipes at our house and Daddy says sometimes workers leave the front door open, and he didn't want Roscoe to run away, so he asked Grammy if Roscoe could visit her house."

"Grammy said yes, even though I don't think she and Papa like Roscoe much."

"They like Roscoe," Logan argued. "They just don't like his fur on the couch."

Faith didn't know Tom's parents beyond exchanging polite greetings, but his mom, Elena, was the most successful realtor in the area, according to her advertisements in the local paper, and his dad, Roberto, was a lawyer of some sort. They'd never come into the antiques shop, to her knowledge.

"Maybe they're allergic to dogs. That's why I didn't have a pet when I was growing up. My mom is allergic to cats."

"But you have a cat now." Nora created another tower of pennies.

"I sure do." Wherever Bettina was now—maybe she'd gone upstairs to her plush bed. "I never actually held a cat until Bettina, because I always worried I'd make my mom cough and sneeze if I had fur or dander on my clothes. But my friend Kellan, from the bookstore? He found these kittens that needed homes, and once I held Bettina, I couldn't tell her goodbye. My mom lives far enough away that I don't have to worry about Bettina making her sick."

"Roscoe doesn't make us sick." Logan shifted on the chair. "I hope he feels better fast."

"Me, too." Faith leaned back. "You know what helps when I'm worried? I ask God for help. Shall we pray?"

Nora nodded and folded her little hands under her chin. Logan bowed his head. Faith shut her eyes and prayed aloud for God to comfort and heal Roscoe, and help the veterinarian to diagnose his ailment.

"Amen," the twins echoed her, one after another.

Faith asked them about their first day in their new kindergarten classes yesterday while they worked. After a while, Nora reached for more coins, but something made her stick her tongue out. "This one's gross."

"Let me see." Faith pulled the quarter closer with her fingertip. It was sticky and partially coated with once-white paper. Most people would toss a coin like this, or spend it as fast as possible, but sometimes guck hid treasures. She scraped at the tacky stuff with her fingernail and uncovered an image of a Revolutionary figure playing a drum. "Look, guys. A bicentennial quarter."

Logan hopped up. "Is it worth a million dollars?"

"No, it's worth a quarter. But it's neat, anyway."

"Why?" Logan peered at it.

"It commemorates the anniversary of American independence." Faith explained about the Bicentennial in 1976. "It may not be worth more than twenty-five cents, but whenever I see one of these, it reminds me of an important event in history. That's a treasure, even if it's not a million dollars."

Logan didn't look convinced, which made Faith laugh. "Yeah, a million dollars could be nice, too. Anyway, we're almost done here. While you two finish, shall I get us a snack?"

"What kind of snack?" Logan's eyes widened.

"I have cookies. How does that sound?"

"Are they chocolate?"

"Chocolate chip."

"Okay, then."

"What if a customer comes in?" Nora looked worried. "Should I sell them a chair?"

"Thanks, but I don't think we need to worry about it. The rain seems to be keeping customers off Main Street today. If someone comes, though, I'll hear the door and I'll be right out."

"Good." Nora sighed in relief. "I don't know how to use the credit card thing yet."

Biting back a grin, Faith washed up at the sink and prepared a small paper plate of cookies—two for each of them. In the cupboard where she kept her tea and sugar, she pulled out a canister of instant lemonade mix. Not her favorite, but the kids would indubitably like it better than the hot tea in the urn. Hopefully, Tom wouldn't mind her plying his kids with sugar.

She didn't always know what to do with kids, but when she was young, she'd loved sorting buttons and coins with her grandma, which gave her the idea for this "job" today. The kids seemed to like it, too. They were sweet. Funny. Weird how she was so at odds with their bossy dad, but she felt nothing but warm fuzzies for the twins.

She carried out a small pitcher of lemonade, three paper cups and the plate of cookies. "Here we are. Do you guys want to wash up first? Some of those coins were grimy. Oh, Bettina's back." The cat was sitting on Nora's lap, eyes half shut in pleasure as the little girl rubbed the top of her head.

"I told her about Roscoe, and she's worried about him, too," Nora said.

"Can we go to the big boulder after our snack?" Logan glanced out at the rain.

"I think we'd better stay here. You like the boulder, though?"

"It's in the park and I want to climb it and be king of it," he said, as if Faith didn't know about the big rock in Hughes Park. It was the very thing that gave the creek its widow's peak, after all. His enthusiasm was infectious, though.

"That'd be fun, but I don't think we're supposed to climb it."

"I want to make my toy cars drive down it."

"Maybe your dad can help you make a ramp for your cars sometime. It'd be smaller, but still fun. Now, do you want a cookie?"

Logan stood up, presumably to go wash. "Where's the bathroom?"

"Right through there." Faith pointed. "Want to go wash up as well, Nora?"

"In a minute." Nora continued petting the cat. "You know what, Miss Faith?"

"What?" Faith took a cookie and savored the chocolate chunks in it. Her favorite.

"Roscoe and Bettina are friends, right?"

The cat and dog had met one time, but who was she to argue? "They did seem to get along pretty well."

"Roscoe didn't bark, and Bettina didn't scratch. And they're a dog and a cat." Nora emphasized the nouns. "They're supposed to fight. You and Daddy fight because you both want the store next door, but maybe you should be friends like Roscoe and Bettina."

Shame filled Faith's throat, leaving little room for another bite of cookie. She'd known the kids had heard the stuff about him not being nice, but she'd hoped they didn't quite comprehend the magnitude of her and Tom's disagreement.

There went that idea.

Embarrassment flooded her cheeks with heat. Not because she was wrong to be upset that Tom had tried to ramrod her about the schoolhouse, no sir, but because she'd lost her temper in front of his kids. She'd said some things that weren't too charitable, too. So had he, but she couldn't control others' actions, and she'd not modeled the best behavior for the kids.

Faith scraped for words to say, even as Logan returned, smelling like lavender hand soap. She took a gulp of lukewarm lemonade, hoping it would loosen the tightness in her throat, but she was saved by the store door opening. Tom already?

Nope, although the woman in the rain-spattered fuchsia pantsuit shared Tom's wavy black hair and cautious expression as she entered the store.

"Grammy!" Nora shouted, sending Bettina scurrying from her lap.

Elena Santos held her arms out to her grandkids. "Hello, darlings. Playing tea party?"

"No way." Logan grimaced. "I don't do that."

"It's a lemonade party, Grammy," Nora corrected.

"They've been big helpers." Faith extended her hand. "Hi, I'm Faith."

"Elena. So nice of you to watch the kids for Tom. He asked me to come get them. He said he'd text you."

Faith withdrew her phone from her pocket. "Not yet, but I'll text him just to let him know—oh, here it is." The message appeared. "My mom is coming to get the kids. Roscoe is improving already. Thanks again," she read aloud.

Another text followed.

I'm sorry for causing offense. My only excuse is trying to do what I think is right for my kids, but I went too far. And for that, I'm sorry.

"Sorry to trouble you, Faith." Elena's comment drew Faith's attention from her phone. With brisk motions, she assisted the kids into their jackets.

"It was no trouble. We had a good time, didn't we?"

"Tell Bettina bye." Nora rushed to Faith, arms extended. Faith bent to hug the little girl. Wow, Nora gave her all in this hug, squeezing so hard it pinched Faith's ribs.

"Yeah," Logan echoed. "Tell her bye."

Faith didn't initiate a hug. It was Logan's choice, and she respected whatever boundaries he needed. But then the shy little boy was in her arms where his sister had been, curled against her side. His embrace was nothing like Nora's. No pressure, just closeness, like he didn't want a hug, necessarily, but to be held.

Her heart felt like it was going to explode at the kids' hugs. No wonder Tom went overboard today in the name of love for these sweet kids.

"Come on, Logan." Elena opened the door, admitting a chill. And then Logan and Nora were gone, leaving a yawning emptiness in the store, as well as Faith's stomach. It wasn't hunger. It was something else entirely.

Grief at how she'd handled things in front of Tom's kids. Gratitude for Tom's apology, even though it was brief and over text, but what more could she expect from a guy with a sick dog at the vet? She appreciated the gesture, but at the same time she felt a total lack of closure between them.

Faith blew a strand of hair from her eyes. She needed to apologize, too, and close this unpleasant chapter. It was the right thing to do, but she was not looking forward to it at all.

After dinner, Tom sat cross-legged on the plush gray living room rug, losing at the kids' favorite board game. Faint rays of sunshine broke through the remaining clouds outside, casting a pale light through the tall windows that overlooked the creek, but it was dim enough that they needed lamplight to play the game of Operation set on the living room coffee table. Squinting, he held the metal tweezers steady as he pinched the plastic "hangnail" and gently withdrew it from the cavity cut into the Operation Sam game board.

Success. No touching the sides, no awful buzz or making Sam's nose glow red. He made an exaggerated show of wiping his forehead in relief. "Phew, that was close."

Logan's turn. "I have to do the heartburn? That one's hard."

"You've got this."

Logan squinted and went for the little plastic heart in Sam's chest. Watching his son, Tom tried to be mindful of times like these, quiet, everyday type moments when he and the kids were together making memories.

"My turn." Nora grabbed the tongs and went for the plastic piece in the rumbling tummy. Despite her care, the game board buzzed, and Sam's nose glowed bright red. Nora shrieked in a dramatic display of mock despair.

Roscoe woke from his nap on the large dog bed by the hearth, blinking at them. Then his ear perked up, clueing Tom into a noise outside a full ten seconds before the doorbell rang.

"Glad to see you're feeling better, buddy." Tom rose to get the door, the hardwood floor off the rug cool on his bare feet. Maybe the plumber forgot something when he was here, fixing the bathroom pipes—a job way beyond Tom's ability. Tom peeked through the peephole and felt his lips part in surprise.

What was she doing here? He opened the door. "Faith."

"Good evening, Tom." She tried to smile but couldn't quite do it. "I'm sorry to drop by unannounced, but I wanted to thank you for your text and at the same time apologize for my words and behavior today, and I, uh— here." She thrust a vintage-looking tin at him. "Three types of fudge. They're not poison or anything. I mean, because of our disagreement earlier—this is not coming out right." She rubbed her head. "Can I start again?"

"Come on in." Tom stepped back, biting back a smile. It seemed she was no more comfortable with how they'd left things than he was.

Her heeled boots clacked on the floor as she entered, accompanied by a tinge of crisp evening air. "How's Roscoe?"

"Miss Faith!" Logan ran into the foyer, Nora at his heels.

"Roscoe's okay," he answered over the kids' heads. "Turns out my mom gave him leftovers. Bellyache is much better now."

Nora twirled around Faith. "How did you find our house?"

"Your dad mentioned you were living in the Millers' old house."

Tom had forgotten that conversation. She took a half step farther inside, not as if she were making herself at home but to look around her at the foyer, two-stories high, flanked by the staircase and lit by a modern-cut glass chandelier. Her gaze took in the updates he'd made, from the dark wood floors to the neutral paint to the new front door. "This sure doesn't look the same as the last time I was here. Wow, Tom, this is beautiful."

A far cry from the tenor of their earlier discussion today. "Thanks."

"We put up pictures and lights," Nora said.

"And painted our bedrooms. Mine's blue." Logan looked at the tin in Tom's hands. "What's that?"

Faith tipped her head toward the tin. "A welcome-to-town gift."

Not necessary. "You gave the kids a book, remember?"

"Then it's an I'm-sorry-for-barking gift." She shoved her hands in the pockets of her houndstooth peacoat.

"You didn't bark. But I'm sorry, too. I messed up." It couldn't have been easy for her to come here after their heated exchange today. With a gift, no less. An unpoisoned one.

He hadn't realized he was smiling until she offered a wary grin. "What's so funny?"

"Just looking forward to the fudge. Three types, you said?"

"Chocolate, vanilla and peppermint cocoa."

"Come in and sample it with us, then."

"Oh, I couldn't." Faith took a half step back. "I'm interrupting."

"We don't mind a break." Tom beckoned her in. "Sorry, can I take your coat?"

"I'll leave it here by the door." She shed her coat and dropped it and her purse on the armrest of the couch in the living room. "I won't stay long."

Hopefully, long enough to have a decent talk. He wouldn't mind a chance to more fully explain himself. Maybe once the kids got going on the fudge, he and Faith could have a few minutes of frank discussion.

He opened the tin, releasing the delectable aroma of rich chocolate and cream. His mouth watered. "A bite for you guys and the rest for me," he teased.

The kids protested while Faith knelt at Roscoe's side

and rubbed his neck, ears and back. "Feeling better, eh? Poor pup."

"Thanks for the vet recommendation." Tom passed paper napkins to his kids. "She was great."

"Peyton's wonderful." Faith rose and folded her arms. "So how's the fudge?"

Tom gave a thumbs-up, unable to answer around the food in his mouth. Wow, she was a good cook. Or baker. Did one bake fudge? Tom's repertoire had been limited to barbecue until this last year, but he was learning. He'd have to learn how to make this.

"Which flavor's your favorite?" Nora pointed at the options.

"I like them all, but...chocolate." Faith smiled at the kids.

The doorbell rang again, causing Roscoe to lift his head and Tom to hold back from taking another bite. "Maybe that's the plumber. Just a minute."

His peephole peek revealed his mother instead of the plumber, though. He swung the door open and kissed her floral-scented cheek. "What brings you out here?"

She gripped his gray sweatshirt, holding him close enough so he could hear her whisper. "Whose car is that out front?"

"Faith Latham."

"The antiques woman? What's going on, Tom?"

"Nothing. *Nothing*," he added, as realization dawned as to why his mother was asking. Faith was not here because there was anything the least bit romantic going on. "You know she and I are competing for the same storefront, and we lost our cools today in front of the kids." At his mom's horrified expression, Tom moved his hands in a settle-down gesture. "Not bad, Mom, okay? But she's here to apologize. That's it."

"I hope that's all, *mijo,* because the last thing my precious grandkids need is to be confused about your relationship with a woman. They've been through enough."

He didn't need his mom's guilt right now. Or her automatic assumption he was interested in dating. "You know I won't date, Mom. Faith is going to be my neighbor on Main Street, though, and this competition over the old livery didn't bring out the best in either of us today. That's all, okay? But that's not why you came. What's wrong?"

"I showed a house in your neighborhood and noticed the strange car. I had to make sure you weren't making a mistake already."

Well, that was a punch in the gut. One week in his own home and his mom thought he'd be neglecting his kids somehow?

"Grammy?" Nora slunk around the corner from the living room. "Why don't you come in all the way?"

Mom grasped Nora in a bear hug. "We're talking grown-up stuff first."

"Are you almost done? We're eating Miss Faith's fudge and it's really good."

"I'll try a nibble." Mom took Nora's hand and led the way to the living room.

"Mrs. Santos." Faith rose from the floor where she and Logan were patting Roscoe. Tom would have thought she was entirely relaxed, except for the bob of her throat, visible beneath her green turtleneck.

This wasn't the easiest situation, and he hadn't helped it any by whispering in the foyer with his mom. She glanced at her coat, a sure sign she was ready to leave, but he wanted to talk to her. To make peace, and maybe his mom's arrival could actually help that happen.

"I'm going to take Roscoe out back. Faith, why don't you come with me so you can see the creek? Mom, you can take my spot at Operation."

At the words *out back*, the feel of the room changed. Roscoe rose and trotted to the sliding glass door. Faith's eyes went wide. Mom's chin lowered, like a bull about to charge. Logan stripped his socks. "I wanna go outside."

"Not this time. Miss Faith and I need to talk about the store, okay, bud?"

"Grown-ups." Nora sighed dramatically. "They always have to talk without us."

Mom shook her head in obvious exasperation, but it wasn't like he was a teenager looking for an excuse to steal a smooch with his first girlfriend. He'd made his intentions clear, and Faith seemed to get that he wanted to talk, because she nodded. "Good idea."

Removing Roscoe's leash from a hook by the sliding glass door, Tom gauged the thickness of Faith's turtleneck. The rain had cooled things considerably today. He was snug in his dark gray sweatshirt, but he ran hot. "Need your coat?"

"No, it'll be all right." Faith preceded him out onto the covered patio.

He slid the door shut behind them. "I hope you don't mind, but I thought it would be good to clear the air without an audience."

"I appreciate it." Despite her insistence that she'd be warm enough without her coat, she folded her arms as if chilled as they trudged over the grassy backyard. "Earlier today, I talked to your kids about how we should say sorry, but then I didn't give you the courtesy of apologizing for some of the things I said. So here it is—I'm sorry, Tom. I shouldn't have insinuated you were trying to bribe me or you were stealing something that isn't even mine. I was upset—I *am* upset—but Nora made me realize I shouldn't have let things get to that point."

"Nora?" He opened the waist-high white picket gate separating his property from the bank of the creek. "Did she say something out of line?"

"Not at all." Faith smiled at Roscoe, who tugged them toward the watery edge of the bubbling creek. "She said Roscoe and Bettina are friends, despite the tendency of their species to fight, though I know plenty of dogs and cats that get along. Anyway, she hoped you and I could be friends like our pets."

Tom's heart swelled in his chest. "That's really cute."

"It is. And wise. So here I am." Faith's green eyes took a mossy hue in the fading sunlight. "I'm not happy about our situation, and I'm not going to give in. But if you win the building, we'll be neighbors, and I'd rather we be friendly ones."

Tom stopped walking as Roscoe stretched to investigate the wild grasses growing at the creek's edge. "Me, too. But I pushed you today, so it's no wonder you got upset. I didn't realize how my words would sound. I'm accustomed to my old marketing job, being assertive with clients, pressuring and looking for alternatives, doing what I have to do to achieve the desired end. God's refining me in a lot of areas, but this one hasn't been tempered well yet. I guess, in my quest to find a solution that would be good for both of us, I totally ignored your need for a space by your store. And I definitely didn't mean to suggest Faith's Finds isn't successful or that you can't handle two businesses. I crossed the line."

It had been bothering him all evening.

"We both said things we regret."

"I sure did. I'm sorry."

"It's okay. I think we're good now." She looked across the creek, and for a minute the only sounds were Roscoe slurping from the creek and the jangling of his tag. "We both have our reasons for passionately fighting for that storefront."

"Is there another reason you want that space? Something I should know about?"

He expected a quick denial, but instead she sighed. "Nothing big, no."

"But something."

She nodded. "Something."

At that moment, he wanted to be there for her. To support her. To be her friend.

Something he hadn't felt with a woman in a long, long time.

His parents wouldn't like it, but there was nothing wrong with being friends with a woman. Even if it was a woman like Faith whose heart was even prettier than her features. He wouldn't mess up.

"Tell me, Faith. What am I missing?"

Chapter Six

Should she tell him? Faith contemplated her words as she toed her boot into the gravelly sand. The setting sunlight dappled the trees and shimmered gold on the creek, and all around was the fresh after-rain smell of green things. "This is a peaceful spot, you know?"

"I missed this place." Tom took a few slow steps away to allow Roscoe to explore, but he maintained eye contact with her, affirming that he was listening. "I didn't know how much until I saw this house, with the creek running behind it and the woods on the other side."

"This town means everything to me."

"It's your home."

"It really is, Tom, and not just because I spent most of my growing-up years here. You know my parents divorced and we moved away. If you checked me out in the yearbook to refresh your memory of me, you'll remember I didn't exactly fit in when I was a kid. Not just in high school, either, so it wasn't like I had an idyllic childhood. It was actually visiting my grandparents here, after we moved away, that gave me the foundation of my life. My faith. Who I am and what I want."

"Like the museum."

"Indirectly, yes. They gave me an appreciation of the past. Every object in their house had a purpose and a story, and they cherished what they had as blessings. Compared to my parents, who chased new things all the time—cars, toys and eventually spouses—my grandparents were the most stable people in my life. I craved their strength and steadiness and the example they led by living with an appreciation of this town and its stories."

"I didn't know your grandparents, but they sound like special people."

"They were. They were the ones who encouraged me to have my store, and I had just moved into the apartment above it when my grandpa passed. Grandma had died the year before. I know they'd be happy for me, though, waking up each day and coming downstairs for a day of fun that I hate to call work. Running a business out of a hundred-and-seventy-year-old building isn't always easy, of course, but it's what I always wanted since I was little. For a few years now that dream has included the museum next door." She'd even been practicing how to answer the phone once she ran both establishments: *Faith's Finds and the Widow's Peak Creek Community Museum. How may I help you?*

Tom took another step, giving Roscoe the freedom to sniff a new tree. "So this isn't just about your wanting a town museum. This is about you honoring your family and the legacy your grandparents left you, a legacy of history. Your past is like home. That's where we differ, I guess, because my past is full of regret, so I'm running toward the future as fast as I can."

"I'm so sorry for your loss, Tom."

"Thanks, but that's not entirely what I meant. I was a lousy father, Faith. And husband. Never around. My career took all my time, and that's how Lourdes and I decided it would be. She wanted financial stability, even if it meant I was gone a lot. And I was. I missed everything. But I can't be that man anymore."

Her chest ached for him. "That's a lot to deal with, Tom. I'm sorry."

"It hasn't been easy, that's for sure, but I started taking the kids to church a year ago." His gaze unfocused at the memory as they walked slowly along the bank. "I was welcomed, cared for and prayed for. I saw God had a plan for me and the kids, and eventually I discerned that I had to come back home where my parents could help me care for Logan and Nora. I feel drawn to help the town, too."

"Catering to tourists and chasing tax dollars like Mayor Hughes wants?"

"Adding to the town's income isn't a bad thing."

"No, but the mayor is so focused on the town becoming something else, like a resort town, I'm concerned she'll work to withdraw protection for the historic buildings on Main Street. They'll end up like the old schoolhouse, dilapidated and ignored."

"I don't think anyone here would allow that to happen. And if someone tried, I'd fight alongside you to preserve the buildings. They're special. That's why I'm all for your museum. Just in the schoolhouse." His full lips twitched.

To her surprise, she laughed. "You and that schoolhouse."

"You can't blame me for trying." His smile widened. "But you have to admit, the town could use an influx of tax revenue. I've looked at the past few years' budgets online, and the town is starting to decline. Tourists aren't coming the way they used to. You said this is a slow season."

"That doesn't mean I'm floundering. I'm selling pieces like the game table to Willa at the Cordova Inn."

"Do you have a website to cater to folks outside of town?"

She'd been thinking about it, but no. "Willa dropped in here and that's how this relationship got started. I'm sure she'd buy more, but her inn is a funky sort of place. Eclectic pieces, but it's important to their guests to have modern conveniences, technology accommodations, that sort of thing."

"Huh." He stared at the horizon.

"What do you mean, huh? You think I need a website, I take it."

"Yes, but that's not what I meant." He faced her, wiggling his brows.

"I'm not sure I like the sound of this. Do you want me to put the museum online or something?"

"This has nothing to do with the museum. This is about Faith's Finds. You."

Her? And why was he looking at her like that, with a boyish grin that made his eyes crinkle and oh, my, he had dimpled cheeks. She'd never noticed those before. His dark eyes fixed on her with such happy intensity that she couldn't look away. Couldn't even fumble out a word.

Spit something out, Latham. Fast.

"Huh?" she managed.

Brilliant.

He laughed. "Let's head back to the house. I'll fill you in on the way, but your future is going to be a lot brighter soon. Trust me."

At Faith's quizzical look, Tom grinned. "Willa wants interesting pieces of furniture for her inn that also fit with twenty-first century living, right? Accommodate technology, you said. So do it. Refurbish antique pieces to work with modern conveniences. That's why I said *brighter*, get it?" Tom led her through the gate into the backyard. Unclipping the leash from Roscoe's collar as he walked, he watched Faith for her reaction to his pun. "Because of the electricity. *Lights*."

Instead of laughing, her brow furrowed like he was rambling crazy talk. "You think I should put lamps into antique furnishings."

He must have really blown the joke. "*Modify* them." He opened the sliding glass door and let them back inside the house. "To accommodate technology. Add places for plugs or outlets. I'm sure your friend Willa would love that."

"Once I modify something beyond preservation, it wrecks the value."

"I'm not suggesting refurbishing something of great worth, Faith. But if you've got a desk sitting around that needs serious refinishing anyway, what harm would it do to cut a small discreet piece somewhere to lodge an outlet? So a hotel guest can charge his phone or laptop or whatever? I know when I was traveling for work, I hated it if the only outlets in my hotel rooms were by the bed and in the bathroom. Wouldn't it be fabulous to put existing furniture to use like that?"

Nora stood from the board game on the floor. "What are you talking about?"

"Furniture. But also, Faith didn't laugh at my joke."

"What joke?" Faith's lips twitched. "That awful pun, you mean?"

He mocked outrage. "My pun was clever."

"I guess it was somewhat de-*light*-ful." Faith rolled her eyes at her own joke.

Tom clapped. "That's the spirit."

Mom's lips set in a grim line. "What's gotten into you?"

Clearing the air, apologizing, moving on—how could he not feel better? In fact, he felt more hopeful than he had in a long time. "I'm a dad. It's my job to make dad jokes."

Mom's eyes narrowed. "I'll take the kids' knock-knock jokes, thanks."

"Knock-knock, Grammy." Logan knocked on his grandmother's knee.

Tom laughed. "Here we go."

Faith turned to listen to Logan's joke, but Tom still wanted to talk about the prospect of altering furniture. It sounded like she had a guaranteed customer in Willa, but if the altered furniture caught on, it could be a boon to her business.

The smallest of touches on her sleeve, and he had her full attention. The weight of their locked gazes was so heavy he felt it in his chest, so he dropped his hand from her arm—surely, his mom would approve—and focused on what he wanted to say. "I'm sure there's a market for restored furniture like that. Or there could be. Think about it."

"I will. I don't love the idea of messing with vintage items, but I can see the merit. Thank you." She broke their eye contact and moved toward the kids. "I'd better get going."

"Did you have a nice walk?" Mom's innocent tone couldn't hide her immense curiosity as to what had transpired.

"We did." Faith donned her coat. "I haven't enjoyed a good stroll along the creek in too long."

"You like to walk outdoors? So do we." Nora scooted on her knees.

"I'd imagine so, since your daddy is opening an out-door gear store."

"We're walking with Roscoe next Saturday up in the foothills." Logan rolled onto his tummy. "Do you want to come with us?"

Tom's stomach flopped. "Miss Faith probably has other plans for Saturday." It was the best he could think of to give Faith an out. They'd moved past their disagreement, sure, and it seemed clear they both wanted to be neighborly in the future, but that didn't mean spending any more time together.

Nora shook her head. "Miss Angie had a date today so Miss Faith worked, but they take turns. Maybe Miss Angie will work in the store so Miss Faith can go on a date with us."

"It wouldn't be a date," Tom blurted.

"Please come." Logan's gaze fixed on Faith, his request soft but clear.

Faith gripped her purse. "It sounds like family time, though."

"Please?" Nora batted her eyelashes.

Logan scooched to his knees and darted to Faith. "I want you come."

Faith met Tom's gaze. He didn't want her to be pressured by his kids, but at the same time, maybe this wouldn't be a bad thing. Strengthen their next-door-neighbor relationship. "You're more than welcome, if you want."

Besides, once she went on the hike and saw the area's value for outside activity, she'd probably be more willing to yield the old livery for a store catering to outdoor pursuits. In the meantime, he'd keep thinking of places she could put her museum that were close enough for her to handle with her store.

It wasn't until after she nodded that he realized he'd been holding his breath.

Faith hadn't been gone two minutes before his mom decided to follow suit. She shook her head at Tom when he walked her to her car. "You're pushing things, Tom."

"I'm not doing anything wrong. This isn't a date. Or a prelude to a date. The kids asked, and how could she say no? How could I?"

"Like this—no." Mom got into her car.

"I can't do that without looking like a jerk," he called after her moving car. But it was true. He couldn't just disinvite someone from a hike.

When he returned to the living room, he investigated the game board. Looked like Mom hadn't played with them more than a turn or two. "Shall we finish this up? I don't know about you guys, but I'm ready for early bed tonight."

The twins groaned. "Da-d-dy." Nora drew out his name to three syllables.

He tweaked her earlobe so she knew he was teasing, but honestly he wouldn't mind a time of quiet contemplation before bed. Today had been a surprise, from start to finish. A roller coaster, with a better ending than he'd expected, but the ride wasn't over yet. Not where Faith was concerned since neither of them was ceding the storefront to the other.

It would be easier if Faith wasn't so…likable. She had character, bringing over a treat tonight to apologize, and she had guts, standing up for what she wanted.

And she was good with his twins. What parent wouldn't appreciate a person being nice to his kids?

"Can I have more fudge?" Logan still had flecks of chocolate on his lips.

"I think you've had enough."

"Maybe you can bring some to school for my birthday."

"Your birthday is my birthday, too," Nora protested.

Tom took his turn at the game. "Sure. Did someone in class have a birthday?"

"Connor." Logan flopped to his stomach and rested his chin in his fists. "His mommy brought cookies."

"I see. But you want fudge." Tom smiled.

"And a mommy."

Tom reached out to rub his boy's narrow back. "I miss Mommy, too, bud."

"When can we get a new one?" Logan looked up.

"A new mom?" Tom gulped.

"Yeah." Nora scooted closer to Tom. "I want a mommy."

They were six. They couldn't possibly understand what they were asking, or that there was no replacing one mom with another. It was natural for them to want a mother, though. "It's not a simple thing, guys. You can't just order one off the internet."

"We know that, Daddy." Nora sounded sixteen.

"I'm gonna ask God for a mom," Logan insisted.

God wouldn't give them one, though. Not when Tom had promised God, himself and his parents there would be no women in his life.

They could pray all they wanted, but Tom wasn't going down that road again.

Chapter Seven

The next Saturday morning before the store opened,
Faith measured out Bettina's dry food for the day and
trekked down the red carpeted stairs to the store. Angie
was swiping the counter with a rag and bleach cleaner
and doing so with such vigor it made the hem of her green
floral dress flutter.

"Everything okay, Angie?"

"I'm fine, but you? I'm not sure you're in your right
mind, fraternizing with the enemy camp."

Ah. She wasn't thrilled Faith was going on a hike
with Tom and the kids today. "That's ironic, considering you've gone on dates with his friend Ender. And I'm
not fraternizing. This isn't a date. It's not even a friend
thing." Faith brushed gray cat hairs from her peach-
colored hooded sweatshirt, the only thing in her dresser
that said "casual outdoor activity" but didn't make her
look like she was headed for the gym. "He's not all bad,
you know. His idea on retrofitting desks and nightstands
to accommodate tech isn't that bad." Although Faith
hadn't looked into it yet.

Angie hooked her thumb back at the wall between the

antiques store and the old livery. "The idea has merit, but I don't want him to make you change your mind about fighting for the space."

"No way am I doing that."

"Good, because this town needs a way to showcase its artifacts. And that place is perfect."

It was nice to hear someone say it, especially since many days had passed and Chloe hadn't even texted an emoji in response to Faith's phone call.

She took Angie into a brief embrace. "Thanks for being on my side."

"Of course." After pulling back, Angie reached to fuss with Faith's hair. "I'm bummed that some of the other shopkeepers are so enthusiastic about Tom getting the building."

"It doesn't mean they don't want a museum or don't like me." Even though sometimes she took it personally and wanted to drown her sorrows in a gallon of mocha-almond-fudge ice cream. "It doesn't mean Tom will sway the council, either. He was talking about doing stuff that could be detrimental to the structural integrity of the store. If he still wants to do that, it could be bad for him."

"Will you bring it up in your presentation for the council?"

She could, but—

"I don't want to sling any more mud. I'm going to focus on the benefits of my museum rather than the drawbacks of his store."

"Civil discourse rather than a shouting match. The world would be a better place if we all adhered to that policy."

Faith glanced at her watch. A minute past ten. She turned the closed sign in the window to open. "The weather's nice, so hopefully we get some customers to make the day go faster for you."

They could use the sales, too, but Faith didn't dare speak it. Much as she didn't want much to change in town, Tom was right about the need for something to draw more visitors to Main Street.

"So where are you going on this hike?" Angie pulled out the feather duster from under the counter and made her way to the window display. Dusting was an everyday part of keeping the store looking its best, but it was never as fun as organizing pieces into displays or getting to know customers.

"Honestly, I don't know. I ran into Tom and the kids in the church parking lot on Sunday. Tom said he'd pick me up here at ten fifteen, and he'd take care of the picnic, too. I haven't seen them around since then."

But she had seen Elena Santos twice. Once at Angel Food, and again at the supermarket when they'd both reached for celery at the same time. After an awkward exchange of you-go-ahead pleases, Elena grabbed her celery and rushed out of the produce section like she didn't want to exchange another syllable of chitchat more with Faith than she had to.

Enemy camps, Angie had said. Well, that explained it. Elena was upset Faith was fighting Tom for the building.

Angie peeked up from dusting the bike display in the front window. "Here comes your hiking group."

Faith swiped her suddenly damp hands on her jean-clad thighs. What did she have to be nervous about? She was going to spend a few hours with cute kids. And their dad. Whom she was battling for a building. Awkward, yes, but nerve-racking? *Just hike and be done with it.*

Dressed in jeans, light jackets and new-looking mini

hiking boots—Nora's tied with fluorescent pink laces—the kids rushed up for hugs, Nora's fierce, Logan's clingy. They smelled faintly of maple syrup. "Hi, guys."

"Hi, Miss Faith."

"Morning." Tom wore jeans and hiking boots, but instead of a jacket he had on a green-and-white-plaid flannel shirt over a casual green button-down.

The Santos trio looked like far more serious hikers than she did in her green canvas tennis shoes. Oh, well. This wasn't a serious hike, right?

Tom tipped his head toward the front door. "Roscoe's out in the car. Are you ready?"

"Sure." Ignoring the fluttering in her belly, Faith grabbed the tiny backpack she was using as a purse, heavier than usual on her shoulder since she'd stuffed it with sunscreen, snacks and water bottles. A quick wave to Angie and they stepped outside. His black SUV was parked just feet away, with a tongue-lolling Roscoe watching them from the back seat.

To her surprise, Tom followed her around to the passenger side of the car. Was he going to help the kids in the back seat, or—oh, my, no one had opened a car door for her since Grandpa. Most men didn't do that anymore, unless they were on a date.

Which this was not. He was showing her courtesy, that's all.

Nevertheless, her nerves buzzed to life at his proximity. He didn't smell like cologne today, but the dark pools of his eyes meeting her gaze created a similar effect on her. Her heart pounded in her throat.

"Thanks," she croaked, taking her seat.

"My pleasure." He shut the door and walked around to the driver's side, whistling, clearly oblivious to the wave of weirdness she'd just experienced. It would be awful if he thought she might be attracted to him.

Which she couldn't be. He was the worst person in the world to have feelings for.

Her nervous system didn't seem to care, though. Each of her senses seemed to be on high alert—making her acutely conscious of the click made by her latching seat belt, the graham-cracker smell of the car, the sudden warmth on her ear—

She twisted in her seat and yelped. Right into Roscoe's doggy face.

Logan cackled. "Roscoe scared you."

"Yeah, I guess he did. Sorry to yell in your ear, Roscoe." Clearly, she wasn't yet as rational as she wanted to be. She scratched the dog behind one ear to hide how jittery her hands were.

She had to get ahold of herself, now, before she did something stupid like letting her knees get all weak again. Tom was a better guy than she'd initially judged him to be, but he was 100 percent completely wrong for her in every single way.

Her knees and nerves would get the message soon enough, if she kept reminding them.

The drive to the parking area near the trail didn't take long to navigate, and the kids were only a few verses into "Old MacDonald" when Tom pulled into a shady spot beneath a live oak tree. "All right, we're here."

"Quack-quack here and quack-quack there," Nora continued singing.

"Where are we going?" Faith reached for the backpack at her feet.

"Mulder Ranch," he said softly, leaning into her so as

not to be overheard by the kids as they noisily unbuckled and continued singing. Or, rather, quacking. "I wanted to keep it a surprise."

Her smile indicated she understood why. Mulder Ranch was another name for the place locals called the daffodil spot. "We could have walked right onto the ranch from the road, you know."

"I thought it might be more fun to hike in through the back way."

"Let's hike," Nora yelled so loud it hurt Tom's ears.

Faith laughed as she tugged an earlobe. "I love your enthusiasm."

While Faith and the kids exited the vehicle with Roscoe, Tom retrieved his backpack, ensuring the picnic lunch, blanket, extra water and dog leash were secure in the pack. He hoisted it over both shoulders. "Let's go."

"Anyone need sunscreen first?" Faith tugged a yellow tube from her little blue pack.

He should've thought of that. "We all do, thanks. You sure you don't mind loaning us some?"

"Don't be silly." She squirted a blob of white lotion into her palm and then handed him the tube. He reached for Logan, who squirmed. "I don't like that stuff."

"Me, neither." Nora grimaced. "It's all coconutty."

Oh, yeah. They hadn't used sunblock since last summer, when they'd had mini tantrums over the stuff for some reason that defied all logic. Tom braced for a fight.

"Too bad," Faith said with a shrug. "I was going to frost you like a cupcake."

Nora did a complete one-eighty, turning her body toward Faith and losing her grimace. "I want to be frosted like a cupcake."

Faith dabbed a dollop onto Nora's nose, which made his daughter squeal.

"Me, me." Logan rushed to Faith's side, nose high in the air. "Frost me like a cupcake."

Faith applied a pea-sized portion on the tip of Logan's nose. He cackled like it was the funniest thing ever. "Now spread the frosting onto your cheeks, too." The kids rubbed their noses while Faith took the tube back from Tom and added more lotion on the tips of their ears and the back of their necks. "Can't forget to frost the edges so the cupcake is as pretty as it is delicious."

And just like that, without a fight, his kids were covered in sunblock. Faith hadn't done anything that earth shattering, but his kids thought it hilarious enough to submit to the sunblock with enthusiasm.

He'd have to remember the cupcake trick next time. Although he had a feeling it wasn't just the trick, it was the woman, who'd not only diffused a potential argument but made the situation fun.

Faith was not like anyone he'd ever met. And even though they were rivals, it seemed the effect she was having on his family was...

Good. Nora was dancing around now, and Logan wasn't acting his usual shy self at all with Faith. Right now, he was poking the dog with a chorus of "boops." Roscoe, of course, took it all in stride, smiling in his doggy way.

Tom smeared some of Faith's sunblock on the back of his neck, breathing in the aroma that always made him feel young and carefree. Like the weight of the world wasn't resting entirely on his shoulders. Maybe the feeling also had something to do with Faith, but he couldn't think of that now. Or at all, really.

This was a hike to cement their neighborly relationship. Nothing more.

Faith shoved the tube back in her pack. "I thought you might be taking us to the Raven Mine, parking out here."

"I didn't realize it was that close." He whistled for Roscoe, who'd gone investigating near a clump of chaparral scrub.

"Quite near Mulder Ranch. There's history everywhere you turn in gold country." Faith grinned as she and Nora preceded him and Logan onto the trail. Roscoe caught up and panted happily as he wove between them.

Nora patted Faith's leg. "Is it called gold country because the grass is yellow?"

"Not quite," Tom answered. It was easy to understand his daughter's question, though, because everything seemed tinged in gold this morning: the warm sunlight, the wild mustard blossoms scattered through the landscape and yes, the yellow hue of the drying grasses. "It's because gold was discovered here a long time ago."

"Right here?" Logan scanned the ground.

"Not on this spot, but close enough that people came from all over the world to look for gold in this area." Faith pointed at the yellow rolling hills ahead. "The Raven Mine is up there. It brought up over three thousand tons of ore one year."

"Is there still gold in there? Can we go?" Logan quickened his pace.

Tom met Faith's gaze. "How far is it?"

"Less than half a mile from the ranch, actually."

"That close? Why didn't I ever go there on a field trip or something?"

"Nothing's left anymore, so some of the other mines

are more interesting to visit. But it's part of the Mine Trail."

"My shoe." Nora wiggled her foot in a circle. Loosened laces flapped around her boot.

Faith paused and dropped to retie it before Tom could even blink. Here she was, helping his kids again. With a tug on the double knot she'd formed, she stood up.

Tom started walking again. "So which came first in 1850-whatever, Main Street or the Raven Mine?"

She grinned. "The Raven wasn't opened until 1869, but Main Street was built in 1852, after gold-bearing quartz deposits were discovered close by. Your ancestor came in '51, I think, but became a mason pretty quickly."

Ah, yes, his great-great-whatever grandfather. "What's your family history here in town?"

"Same as yours, for the most part." She glanced back at him as they continued up the trail. "A few of my ancestors found they made better livings at things like law enforcement, animal husbandry, that sort of thing, but two of my great uncles worked in the Raven. Mining is part of the fabric of this town. We wouldn't be here without it."

"I never thought of it that way."

"Me neither, not in my whole life," Logan said.

It was difficult to keep a straight face at that remark. Faith must have thought so, too, because as they walked she turned back to smile at Tom—

And yelped, falling to her knees.

Tom gripped her arm and tugged her upright, pulling her close to stabilize her. "You okay?"

"Yeah. Sorry, I should've been watching where I was going."

"You landed hard. Do your knees hurt?"

She shook her head, causing her hair to sweep his

hands, which still rested on her shoulders. Their faces were inches apart. So close he could breathe the faint scents of sunblock and laundry soap. Their gazes held, for a moment or an eternity, he couldn't guess.

He forgot where he was. His gaze lowered on its own accord to her peach-glossed lips.

"Daddy, you let go of the leash and now Roscoe's running away," Nora chastised.

What was he doing? "Right. Gotta get Roscoe back." He released Faith and whistled after Roscoe, who trotted back with obvious reluctance.

"You're sure you're all right?" His question was for Faith, but he made a point of not looking into her eyes again.

"Yeah. Just didn't see this rock." She brushed dirt from her knees.

"Are we almost there? I'm hungry." Logan rubbed his stomach.

"Soon, bud." Even though they were taking a roundabout way, Tom hadn't forgotten his kids were kindergarteners. The trek he'd chosen wasn't too long or rigorous.

They talked cartoon movies and plant names and Nora's wayward shoelaces—which mysteriously kept untying themselves despite Faith's double knots—as they made their way up the gentle slope to the daffodil spot. The shallow conversation was perfect, not too personal but easy enough so he and Faith established a neighborly foundation, as intended. Nothing more.

He would not be attracted to Faith. Nope.

He prayed as he walked, begging God's help.

Then the oaks and pines surrounding the trail thinned and a chain-link fence appeared ahead. The gate before them stood open, welcoming. They went through it but stopped at the top of the slope leading down into the backside of Mulder Ranch, private property whose owners welcomed visitors every spring when the daffodils bloomed.

It was better than he remembered. Below, the ranch spread out, dotted with grazing cattle in a half-dozen shades of brown. Glimpses of the owners' white Georgian-style home were barely visible through the barrier of cypress trees planted around it. The Mulders had posted welcome signs, though, directing visitors to take out whatever they brought in and leading them to make themselves at home on the acreage down the slope, where a donkey watched them from a paddock by the old wood barn a hundred yards or so from the banks of the creek.

Between them and the barn, however, were the daffodils. Thousands of them, white and yellow, some fully open to the sun, others still closed tight in yellow-green buds, waving on bright green stalks in the gentle breeze.

"Wow." Logan's mouth went slack.

"It's bee-you-tiful." Nora tucked her clasped hands beneath her chin.

"It really is." Faith led them down the slope. "I'd forgotten just how much."

How could that be possible? She was all about the town's heritage, and this was a part of it. "Aren't these bulbs really old?"

"The tradition is over a hundred years old, so yes, some say many of the bulbs are decades old. The family plants new ones every year, though." She turned to look at him over her shoulder, so pretty his heart stopped for a second. "Thanks for bringing us here, Tom. This is wonderful."

It was. The scenery, and the feeling in his gut. It was as close to happiness as he'd had in a long time.

Just for today, he'd stop worrying about being the perfect dad for his kids to make up for failing them. Or whether or not Faith could be both friend and foe, especially when he was starting to appreciate her a little more than he should.

Just for today, he would choose to enjoy the moment.

Chapter Eight

"Can we pick daffodils?"

"Can we smell them?"

"Can we look at the donkey?"

Tom laughed at the barrage of questions. "No, yes, and yes."

The kids ran down the path through the daffodils toward the donkey, Faith at their heels. Tom leashed Roscoe and dug his phone from his pants pocket to take pictures. He'd have to get a few of the kids among the blooms, too.

After a minute with the donkey, Logan's shoulders slumped. "Can we eat now?"

Tom's stomach rumbled, too. "Sure. How about over there?" He pointed to a flat spot beneath a wide old oak.

First things first. He removed a collapsible pet bowl from his pack and poured the contents of a water bottle in it for Roscoe. While the dog lapped in noisy slurps, he and Faith laid out a gray blanket. After wiping their hands with a towelette, they said grace and dug into their ham-and-Swiss sandwiches.

"That is one snazzy backpack. My picnic basket belonged to my grandparents. I love it, but it doesn't insulate like yours does. Or have as many nifty compartments." Faith munched on a tortilla chip, eyeing his backpack.

"I'm going to carry them in my store, for sure. They're lightweight and hold a lot of stuff." He glanced at her sandwich. "Hope you don't mind ham and cheese. Or sourdough."

"It's one of my favorites, actually. This is from Sweet Pickles, isn't it?"

"Best deli in town."

"The only deli in town."

Nora wiped her hand on her pants. "We bought sandwiches, but brought everything else from home. I washed the apples."

"And I put the chips in baggies." Logan helped himself to a few more.

"You guys did a great job."

"We're good helpers, just like with the coins," Nora reminded her.

"That you are."

Since they started eating, a few other families had pulled in from the road to visit the daffodil spot. One included a pair of grandparents, and the groups took photographs amongst the flowers. Tom didn't recognize them, but this was the sort of place where everyone was a neighbor, waving and exchanging happy words about the daffodils and the beauty of the day.

It was one of the reasons he'd moved home, so his kids could experience this type of community.

One of the other children pulled a yellow kite from a bag. Nora sat up straight. "I'm done eating. May I go watch the kite?"

"Yeah." Logan swiped his mouth with his paper napkin. "Can we?"

May we, can we. Tom would have to work on that with the kids. "Go ahead. Don't go out of sight, though."

Faith watched them run down the slope. "Nora seems happy. Logan's less shy these days, too, with me, anyway. How was their first full week of school?"

"Great. Nora loves everything. Logan's less effusive, but he's talked about two boys by name this week. I think he's getting more comfortable living here." He was certainly comfortable praying for a new mom every night at bedtime. Tom wasn't going to mention that to Faith, though.

"I'm glad the kids are settling in well. They're sweethearts."

"I kinda like them, too," he teased, stroking Roscoe as the dog stretched on the blanket. "They were my only reason for getting up in the morning for a while. They're why I first went to church, because I realized I needed God to help me raise them. Now my parents are coming to church, too."

"It's wonderful how God works sometimes." She plucked a blade of grass, sending the sweet aroma into the air. "My grandparents were the ones who first introduced me to God and helped me on my faith journey."

"No wonder you feel so strongly about them and preserving Widow's Peak Creek. You're honoring the people who loved you unconditionally, aren't you?"

Her shy smile was as becoming as her other smiles were. "I think they'd be proud of Faith's Finds."

"I'm sure your parents are, too."

"They don't love antiques or go to church, sorry to say." Her head shook. "I pray for them, though."

"That's one of the best things you can do."

A heavy topic, but they were mellow and relaxed on the blanket in the shade. Listening to the kids' laughter and Roscoe's snores, he leaned back and shut his eyes. He breathed deeply of the fresh air, taking in the scents of soil, pine and Roscoe's doggy smell.

And something else, Faith's scent. A faint floral that seemed old-fashioned but timeless. Kind of like her.

"Tom?"

He opened one eye and propped onto his elbow. The kids seemed okay, running around beneath the kite. "Yeah?"

"I think you're right."

"About what?"

Her gaze met his in an earnest, almost abashed way. "Your store."

"Not the *location* of your store," Faith hastened to add, before he thought she might be ceding the property to him. "But the necessity of it. You've said it a hundred times, but I better understand now."

"Oh, yeah?"

From this height, they could view a bend of the creek well enough to see a girl and a man with fishing poles. Faith pointed at them. "They're not going to catch much, but that doesn't matter. They're doing something together. That's what your store will help provide, tools and means for people—families—to spend time together in our beautiful county."

Tom shifted to sit up straighter. "That's my hope. For me and my kids, too. Camping, fishing, it's about fun, sure, but it's also about creating memories."

"Today's already had some great memories." She'd

snapped a few pictures of the kids among the daffodils on her phone. None of Tom, though. It would be too tempting to look at them.

His gaze fixed on his kids, who still lingered by the kid with the kite. "Where's your favorite camping spot around here?"

She could name some sites, but it wouldn't answer his question. "I've never camped."

He sat up. "Never?"

"My parents weren't the camping type, although my mom and her husband have gone *glamping* in the Canadian Rockies, and I've gotta say, it sounds marvelous." Not exactly roughing it, though. "I was supposed to go with the Scouts as a kid, but I got sick."

"I can't believe it." Tom resumed leaning on his elbow. "No campfires, no s'mores?"

"I've had a s'more, but not in the wilderness." Plus, she'd consumed a lot of s'mores ice cream. "I never met a chocolate I didn't like."

"No sleeping bag or food cooked under the stars?"

"No mosquitos or bears, either."

"You've missed out."

"Yeah, maybe." The temperature had warmed up, so she shoved her sleeves up to allow the breeze to brush her forearms. "The past few years, I've been so focused on my store and the museum that I forgot to experience the world outside Main Street. Not that I don't send many people to view the wonders of God's creation here. I just haven't been out here myself in a while."

"The world outside," he echoed. "I like that name for my store, if you don't mind me using it."

"The store you'll have out by the highway?" she teased. "Couldn't help it."

"Very funny." Tom ripped blades from a clump of grass and tossed them at her legs.

It was almost like flirting, but Faith knew better. He was just keeping things light, so she tossed a few blades of grass at his fancy hiking boots.

He shook them off with a twist of his ankle. "Did you have a good week at the store?"

"I did. And I decided to look into your idea of retrofitting furniture. One piece, as a test. A mid-century blond oak piece that's kinda beat up, so it needs a lot of work, anyway. I'm talking to an electrician about it this week."

With his huge grin, he looked just like Logan. "Really?"

"Really. It was a good idea."

He looked a little smug. "I have another idea for you, if you want to hear it."

"No promises, but I'm listening."

"I think you should campaign to save the schoolhouse—"

"Not this again." She wasn't angry, but he needed to let that idea go. She tossed a leaf at him to prove her point.

Flicking it out of his hair, he leaned forward, earnest. "Hear me out. Save it, *not for your museum*, but because it's old and frankly, an eyesore."

"You don't want me to put the museum there anymore?"

"You can't, right? You said it's too small."

He'd listened. She almost whooped. "It's way too small."

"It's also a deterrent to tourism, so I think we should press city council to allocate funds to fix it up, on the outside at least. Put a plaque on it, too. Like I said, I'm good with presentations. What do you say?"

The schoolhouse saved, not for her museum but because it was worthy of preservation. "How could I say no to that?"

He didn't answer, though. His smile didn't change, either. He just stared at her. And she stared back.

Oh, no. What she'd felt in her store when he smelled good, and again in his car when he opened the door for her? Those wild nerves on edge and melty at the same time?

It wasn't going away. It was getting worse.

Tomás Santos, her rival, made her swoony.

Blinking, she fumbled with her water bottle cap and drank down half the water without stopping. Anything to give her an excuse not to look back at him.

Lord, this can't be happening. I cannot like him like that. I don't even know why I would, because he wants my storefront and we don't like any of the same things, even.

Except his kids. And ham sandwiches. And You.

Suddenly, she couldn't keep still. "Do you want to see where the mine is?"

"Oh, yeah." Tom gathered the lunch scraps. "No trash cans here, so we can put our trash into the bag."

She compressed sandwich wrappings into a baggie, sealed it up tight and passed it to him without touching his fingers.

Impressive fine motor skills, there, Latham.

"Kids, time to go," Tom called, rousing Roscoe from his nap.

"Aw," Logan yelled.

"Don't you want to see the mine?"

Logan cast one more wistful glance at the yellow kite before jogging up the slope to join them, Nora at his heels.

"You liked the kite?" she asked.

"Yeah, I want one." Logan took a long drink of water.

The blue kite in Faith's display window was sitting there, unused. It wasn't vintage, but it was so cute she hadn't been able to resist buying it from the local who sold them at the farmer's market. She'd have to buy two more as presents for the twins.

"Why are you smiling, Miss Faith?" Nora wiggled close to her face, nose to nose.

Faith tickled her under the chin. "Kites are fun to watch."

"It'd be funner to watch if I was the one holding the string." Nora's lower lip stuck out. But then her chin lifted, inviting another tickle.

"More fun," Tom corrected.

Logan was in her face now, too, chin up. "Me, me."

Hopefully, Tom didn't mind her tickling the kids. After a minute, though, Faith wobbled as the earth moved beneath them—not the earth. The blanket. Tom held one end and tugged, giving them all a scoot. "Let's go see the mine."

"More ride," Logan demanded.

Faith hopped off the blanket so he could pull the kids around easier. "Real quick and then Daddy and I will fold the blanket."

Tom tugged them a few feet, then shook it like a wave. "Let's go. Everyone's shoelaces tied?"

Sure enough, Nora's had come untied again. Faith gave the double knot a tug and could only laugh when the slick laces started to loosen on their own. "I think you need laces made of a different type of material."

"That's what Daddy says but I wanted the pink ones, so he switched them for me."

The smile she exchanged with Tom sent a flutter through her abdomen, reminding her to get a grip on herself. This…whatever it was, needed to die. On the vine. Like, yesterday.

They backtracked the way they'd come, over the shady path, and then took a fork at a metal sign indicating they were on the Mine Trail. Fewer than a hundred yards later, the oaks thinned and they reached their destination. Faith tapped the metal sign with her fingernail, making a plinking sound. "The Raven Mine."

"Where?" Nora looked up, down and everywhere.

"The buildings aren't here anymore, honey. Everything of value—monetarily and historically—was removed a long time ago. I purchased some artifacts from this site to be exhibited in the town museum, though."

"Why'd we come if nothing's here?" Logan cupped his hands over his eyes to block the bright sun, reminding Faith it had been a while since she applied sunblock.

Reaching in her bag, she beckoned him over. "To see what's left."

"This is part of town history, son. Family history, too. It's important."

"Well I'll be," Faith said, as she frosted the cupcakes that were his children with 50 SPF. "You sound like a history buff, Tom Santos."

"Well, I couldn't tell you a thing about how they mined for gold."

Faith pointed at what was left of the hoist foundation. "That's where they pulled ore from the soil below, and there, where that bit of wood is, is all that's left of the stamp mill."

She offered an explanation of how it had worked, but the kids weren't too interested in the mechanics. They seemed keener to search for gold along the path. It wasn't like there was anything to see, though. Soon the weeds would overtake the site. They were thick and long, brushing against their jeans as they walked. Faith felt a pinch and bent down to pull a barbed sticker from her sock.

"Hey," Tom said, as she dug it out. "Don't get up. You've got a bug on your back."

Faith froze. "A bee? A spider?" Her skin crawled.

"It's big and black." He brushed at her spine between her shoulder blades.

Not a bee, okay, but black widow spiders were black. Did they live out here? Faith's pulse ratcheted. "Is it gone?"

Another brush. "Yes."

She jumped away, swatting at every inch of clothing she could reach. "Are there any more? Any in my hair?"

"Seriously, you're afraid of bugs?" Tom's smile didn't reassure her as he leaned closer to examine her hair. "I don't think so. It was just some weird beetle, maybe."

That was unhelpful. "Aren't you supposed to know what's what out here, Mr. *World Outside*?"

"I'm not a biologist." Cracking a smile, he scanned her hair. "But I think you're safe now."

Safe from weird beetles, maybe, but now that she was out of mortal danger, his closeness caused her bones to melt like wax.

So no, she was not safe—at least her heart wasn't. If she wasn't careful, her heart could be in big trouble.

Chapter Nine

Faith jumped back, as if she were in danger of another big bug landing on her. She had to get a grip on these burgeoning feelings for Tom before she was swept away by them. She also needed to say something to cover the awkwardness. Fast.

"You're going to have to order some flora and fauna books for the store so you can identify beetles better, Tom."

"Yeah," he said a second too late. Like he wasn't unaffected, either.

Nora ran to her dad. "Do I have bugs in my hair? I don't want bugs, Daddy."

Grateful for the diversion, Faith examined Logan's shirt and hair while Tom inspected Nora. "Nope."

"I don't like buggy places." Nora clung to Tom's leg.

"The *world outside* is a buggy place." Faith patted Logan's shoulders. "No bugs on you, though."

"I don't care about bugs, but we should go anyway," Logan said. "There's no gold here."

"Sorry, pal." Tom stepped toward the trail.

The kids led them on the trail back, keeping up a steady stream of chatter while Faith and Tom followed behind with Roscoe. Faith added to the conversation at every opportunity, if only to keep her attention off of her unwelcome feelings for Tom.

It had been a lovely day, but it was for the best they were going home now. She would spend the evening with a book and a mug of herbal tea, glad she and Tom were capable of a civil relationship. And she would force herself to forget all about her kooky response to him.

Nora turned back. "It's slippery right here, Daddy. You'd better help Miss Faith since she almost fell earlier."

Aww, how sweet. "Thanks, Nora. I'm okay, though."

It wasn't quite as sweet two minutes later when Logan pointed at the ground. "Here's a big root, Daddy. Make sure Miss Faith doesn't trip and hurt her knees again."

"You guys are doing a great job warning me of potential dangers. I'll go around it." She did not need Tom's assistance to dodge an inch-high root. When she fell earlier, she'd been looking at him. She'd thoroughly learned her lesson and kept her eyes on the ground ahead of her now.

The kids continued to point out hazards until they reached the end of the trail. On seeing the black SUV in the parking lot, the kids ran ahead.

"Wow, they think I'm a klutz." She glanced at Tom, laughing.

"I guess I should be grateful they're considerate." Tom unlocked the doors with his key fob. The hatchback lifted and Roscoe hopped right in, as if happy to be going on a ride home.

That made two of them. The day had been lovely, the exercise wonderful, but her thoughts and feelings about Tom had been unsettling to say the least. She needed to buckle down this evening and focus on getting the storefront they were battling over.

Without waiting for Tom to get her door, Faith slid into the passenger seat, dodging the bullet of being close to him again. As Tom pulled out of the small paved lot onto Raven Road, she kept her eyes on the scenery and chatted with the kids about the daffodils. When they were about two minutes from her store, Faith shifted to reach for her bag at her feet, ready to hop out as soon as he parked. "Thanks for the fun day. And the sandwich. Delicious."

"I want turkey next time," Logan said.

"Can we have turkey for dinner?" Nora asked.

"I was thinking pizza and veggies tonight, actually." Tom navigated the gentle curve of the road toward the old part of town.

"Pizza?" Logan's voice rose in pitch. "Can Miss Faith come?"

Another invitation by the kids that had blindsided Tom by the look of his parted lips.

Nora leaned forward to tap the back of Faith's seat. "Please, Miss Faith?"

"You need a good dinner," Logan added. "Veggies are good for you."

"And we can play a game. Right, Daddy?"

She'd spare him having to say no to his begging kids. Turning in her seat to decline the offer, she smiled at them with her best apologetic look. "You guys are the best, but—"

Tom sucked in a sharp breath.

"What?" She swiveled back.

Blue and red lights flashed at the southwest corner of Main Street around the area of the creek. People lined the sidewalks, staring at the cloud of dark gray smoke marring the otherwise bright blue sky.

Something was on fire. Or had been, recently enough that there was still a lot of activity going on.

From the back seat, the kids asked more questions than she could untangle, most of which they had no answers to. The moment Tom parked the car in front of her store, Faith unbuckled her seat belt. "I'd better go."

Tom pulled his keys from the ignition. "We're coming, too."

"Are you sure?" She opened her door, admitting the choking odor of smoke into the vehicle. This might not be the best place for kids.

"We'll keep our distance, but I need to know what's going on."

While he leashed Roscoe, she let the kids out, praying all the while no one's home had been lost in that little neighborhood across the bridge, just past the old schoolhouse. *May no one be hurt, Lord. Please.*

They made their way down the street. Faith couldn't see any ambulances, although a police car blocked Main Street between Emerald's Restaurant on the right and DeLuca's Pizza on the left. Two bright red fire department vehicles were parked askew, blocking the bridge over the creek. On the other side of the bridge, a smaller white and red truck had parked, *Fire Investigations* emblazoned on its side.

A few more steps through the gathering crowd and then she could see. The sight robbed her of breath.

The schoolhouse was gone. All that remained was a steaming, smoking pile of charred debris.

Tom's hand went to his mouth.

He gathered the kids closer to him and looked for a familiar face among the crowd. Kellan, the bookstore manager, wasn't too far off. Tom lifted a hand. "Kellan, hey. Was anyone hurt?"

The man with floppy blond curls shook his head as he stepped closer. "No, thank God. This could have been so much worse."

In other words, the rest of Main Street could have burned down, too, endangering lives and destroying livelihoods, as well as historic properties. "Hate to think about it."

"This is unsettling, for sure. Oh, hey, Faith." To Tom's surprise, Kellan enveloped Faith in a one-armed hug. "What a blow."

"It's awful. And your store is just feet from the schoolhouse. I'm so glad God protected you. Do you know what happened?"

Kellan held on a half second too long for Tom's liking. "A cigarette butt in the weeds, maybe? Who knows?"

Faith's eyes welled with tears. "Such a shame."

It was, but all Tom could think of right now was how much it ached to see her face etched in sadness. And he felt a strange, powerful ache, too, not over the schoolhouse, but what could have happened had she been inside it today, had he got his way when he initially suggested she put the museum there.

"I am so sorry, Faith. When I think how hard I pushed you to occupy the schoolhouse, paying no mind to whether or not it was safe?" He wished he'd been the one to hug Faith a few seconds ago. He'd look like an idiot if he did it now.

"To think we'd planned to restore it."

Kellan shook his head. "I didn't know you were thinking of fixing it up."

"We just talked about it a few hours ago. Oh, Maeve."

Faith shifted away to reach out to the ample-figured woman with the gray bobbed hairdo who ran the yarn store. "Can you believe it?"

Maeve hugged Faith hard. "A bit of our history, up in smoke."

The twins shifted against Tom's legs, as if ready to move on. There wasn't much more to be learned here anyway, but Maeve looked at him with sharp blue eyes. "You're Tom Santos, aren't you? I'm Maeve McInnis. I run In Stitches, the yarn store."

"Nice to meet you." He shook Maeve's warm hand. "These are my kids, Logan and Nora."

They shook her hand to his relief. Sometimes his kids weren't always the best at remembering to use good manners, but they were working on it.

Maeve looked like the sort of woman who didn't miss much, and by her appraising glances at him, she'd undoubtedly heard about his and Faith's competition for the old livery up the street. She didn't say a word, though.

Maybe she didn't speak because Kellan couldn't stop talking all of a sudden. "How's Bettina?"

"Sassy. How's Frank?"

"Lazy." They shared a secret sort of laugh.

Faith looked down at the kids. "Bettina and Frank are sister and brother. Kellan is the one who introduced me to Bettina in the first place."

"Is Frank teeny like Bet-teeny?" Nora asked.

"Frank is bigger." Kellan held his hands as if an invisible football had been placed there. "I probably feed him too much."

"Our dog eats a lot but he isn't fat. See?" She patted patient Roscoe on the head.

Maeve grinned. "Your Roscoe reminds me of my old

pooch, Attila. Sweetest dog ever. Say, I have some craft kits in my shop that could use child testing. Could you two help me out so I know how long they take to make?"

Faith met Tom's gaze. "I can take them, if you want. I don't need to see any more of this."

"I don't, either—"

"Say, Tom," Kellan interrupted. "Would you be interested in joining the Wednesday men's Bible study? We meet at six a.m. at Del's Café, right up there." He pointed to the restaurant two doors up from the yarn store.

"We'll see you in a few minutes, Tom." Faith took the kids' hands. "Bye, Kellan."

"Bye, Faith." Kellan brushed a curl off his forehead. "As I was saying, there are a dozen of us from different churches. Good group of guys."

"I'd be interested, sure." Nice to know Kellan was a man of faith, too. Before he could ask more questions, though, he caught sight of his frowning parents weaving their way through the crowd to him and Kellan. Mom's forehead wrinkled and Dad's eyes, so much like Tom's, narrowed into slits. Was this what he looked like when he was perturbed? Scary.

He hugged his parents and introduced them to Kellan, who they knew by sight.

Mom didn't waste time being polite, though. "Tomás, where are my grandchildren?"

"In the yarn store."

"Alone?" Mom started muttering and moving toward In Stitches.

"They're safe with Faith."

His words stopped his mother.

"Faith's great," Kellan added, probably in an effort to reassure Tom's parents that the kids hadn't been sent off with a monster. He had no clue his parents' concern wasn't Faith's ability with kids, but rather the fact that she was a single woman. "Anyway, I'd better get back in the store. I left my teenage helper in there and I don't want to leave her alone too long. See you folks around."

"Bye, then." Tom took a deep breath, bracing for his parents' inevitable scolding. It'd be better if half the town didn't overhear, so he tugged Roscoe's leash and led his parents away from the crowd to the sidewalk by the restaurant. "I can tell you're upset."

Mom didn't answer but pulled her shiny blue and pink shawl tighter around her shoulders. To her, this was casual dress.

Same with Dad's ironed jeans and starched shirt, which were as stiff as his posture. The only thing moving was his mustache, a clue that he was working his jaw— his most telling sign of stress. "Elena told me how the kids invited Faith Latham on the hike, and you couldn't get out of it without being rude, but why are they still with her?"

"Kellan invited me to a Bible study, so I got stuck out here. She and Maeve were really nice to get them out of the smoke."

His mom didn't look relieved. "You promised not to date."

"I'm not. Honest."

"Does she know that?" Mom poked him in the collarbone with a sharp acrylic nail. "If she has designs on you, stuff like this will only encourage her."

That was almost funny. "She does not have designs on me, Mom. Trust me."

"You've got plenty of money, Tom, and a nice house. Of course, she has designs on you."

"You've pegged her all wrong. Things like that aren't important to Faith."

"Rob, you talk to him." Mom rubbed her forehead. "He's not listening to me."

Dad rubbed the back of his neck. "Maybe she has designs, maybe not. But the kids could get attached to her, and you know it's not good for them to bond to someone who will not be a permanent part of their lives."

"If I get the old livery, Faith and I will be next-door neighbors. But even if I don't, she goes to the same church the kids and I do. No matter what, she'll be part of their lives."

"You need to be careful, *mijo*," Mom added. "She seems to be around a lot, and you promised you'd focus on your job as a parent."

"I don't need the reminder about where my priorities lie."

"Don't you?"

"Seriously, I was thinking about it not five minutes ago. And this is not the place to have a discussion like this."

"I don't care where we have this discussion, if you're going to act like you did in San Francisco." Dad's voice was low, but emphatic.

Every single thing in his life was different than it had been in San Francisco. He rubbed his mouth, holding back the first words that leaped to his tongue, praying for new ones.

"Look, I know your concern is based in love for the kids. And for me. But I assure you, I am a hundred percent focused on Logan and Nora. Faith is a friend. Sort of. I mean, this was a good opportunity to set our rivalry aside and show the kids how adults should handle conflict. But that's all it is."

"If you say so." Dad didn't look the least bit convinced.

Maybe it was because Tom himself wasn't so convinced after today. He liked being around Faith more than he should.

But it didn't matter what he felt or thought he felt. There was nothing between him and Faith, or any woman. Not now and not for the foreseeable future.

Right, God? The kids come first. Not Tom's feelings.

"I'm going to get the kids. See you tomorrow. You're coming to church with us, right?"

"Sure." Dad didn't seem thrilled.

Tom forced a smile for Dad, kissed Mom's cheek and tugged Roscoe's leash.

Was the dog welcome in the yarn store, as he was in Faith's shop? Tom let out a frustrated exhalation. He'd have to take him in for a second to get the kids.

He opened the door, stepping into the cozy shop that smelled of wool. Lurking by the door with Roscoe, he searched for Faith and the kids, but they were too deep in the store to spot. He couldn't see Maeve, either, but a redheaded woman to his right poked through bundles of yarn displayed on an aisle endcap. "I'm so glad the schoolhouse is gone," she said to the brunette with her. "Now the restaurant behind it can finally offer creekside patio seating."

"Seriously," her friend said. "There's old-fashioned charm and then there's taking it too far. Like the antiques store. It's like my grandma's garage in there."

Tom's stomach sank. Faith and the kids had been in

the aisle. Faith walked right past the women, but her face was blotchy and pink. She'd heard every word.

"Oh, hi, Faith." The brunette's syrupy tone didn't fool anyone.

"Hi, Rhonda." Faith glanced at Tom and led the kids straight out of the store. Tom and Roscoe followed her quick pace up the sidewalk toward her store. That woman's words must have cut Faith to the quick.

"Faith," he started, catching up to her.

"See our crafts, Daddy?" Nora lifted a lilac-hued fabric pillow for his inspection. "It's for the next time I lose a tooth. I put the tooth in this pocket here so it's safe."

"Here's mine." Logan's pillow was blue. "We stuffed it and Miss Faith sewed mine shut while Miss Maeve sewed Nora's."

"They're great, guys."

"They are." Faith grinned and let go of their hands.

"Faith, can we discuss what just happened in there?" Tom jerked his thumb back at the yarn store. He was so angry he didn't care that the kids could hear this line of discussion. "Those women don't know what they're talking about."

"Everyone's entitled to an opinion." She glanced at the kids, clearly not wanting to say much around them. "And they're right about the schoolhouse. Nothing lasts forever."

"Love does," Nora said.

Faith smiled at that. "You're right. But things? Not so much."

This was a far cry from the Faith who championed preserving the old, the Faith who found a story in the town they lived in, as well as the objects in her store. How could he encourage her?

All he had to go on was his own experience. "This has been a huge disappointment, but it'll all work out. Even when you have no idea how or when."

He was living proof of that. He had no sure answers about his store yet or how he'd manage to raise his kids on his own. But God held the future, and Tom clung to that with all his might.

"You're right. Sometimes it's hard to be patient and wait for God to unfold things, though." Faith didn't meet his gaze. "Thanks for the nice day. I'd better go check in with Angie."

Tom wanted to chase after her. To talk this through. He didn't want their day to end like this.

But with a brisk wave for the kids, she hurried off toward her store.

Chapter Ten

Faith's Finds wasn't just Faith's business, it was also her home. So the moment she entered the shop and took in the familiar scents and sounds of the place—lemon polish, creaking wood floors, the soft whisper of the fan—her shoulders relaxed.

Angie looked up from the computer, anguish in her eyes. "Faith. You know about the schoolhouse?"

"Yeah. It's gone."

Angie gave her a quick hug. "I stepped outside when the firetrucks roared down the street, but I didn't stay out there to watch. Do they know what happened yet?"

"I don't know. I saw the fire investigator's truck, though, so they're looking into the cause."

"It's such a shame." Angie sighed. "The only silver lining to this is you can't put the museum there now, no matter how hard Tom pushes."

"Believe it or not, Tom finally understood that, as well as how neat the schoolhouse was on its own. He offered to help me make a proposal to the city council asking them to restore the schoolhouse for its own sake, because it is—was—part of town history."

"No." Angie's jaw dropped. "Really?"

"Really." Faith rubbed her temple. "Not that it matters now."

"So, other than the fire, your day went okay, then?"

"Great hike, yeah. We visited the daffodil spot at Mulder Ranch, as well as the old Raven Mine. The kids are a hoot." Faith glanced around to see if she could slip upstairs for a few minutes. Customers were few enough that Angie could handle things in here. "I'd like to clean up, if that's all right."

"Of course. I'm leaving right at five tonight, though. Ender is taking me to dinner and a movie."

"Sure." The store closed at five o'clock in the off-season, and Faith didn't need Angie to tidy up.

She let herself through the gold cord on the staircase and marched to the second floor. Each step seemed heavier than the last, and not just because she'd been using different muscles today on the hike.

It was like her heart was sinking.

She'd known for years she was far fonder of antiques than other people were. Her sister, Chloe, and her parents were Exhibits A, B and C. But coming home to the smoldering ruins of the schoolhouse hurt. So did overhearing those women.

Shake it off, Latham. You've been through this before.

At Faith's entrance into her apartment, Bettina's small gray head lifted above the arm of the beige fabric wingback. Faith crossed through the small royal blue–painted foyer to the living area, which she'd decorated in navy and neutral shades. The sleepy cat's eyes narrowed with the confused look of a creature, animal or human, disturbed from deep sleep. It was so cute Faith couldn't help but smile.

Bettina purred as Faith gently rubbed her silky triangular ears. "You make things better, don't you, baby girl?"

That was one thing God had taught Faith when He put Bettina in her life. Pets were a special kind of balm, soothing her wounds on difficult days. She'd never experienced that as a kid, but she was glad for it now. She'd have to thank Kellan again, next time she saw him, for placing Bettina in her arms four years ago.

The Lord had given her so much. A business, a home, a church and friends. Her family might not be the most supportive—Chloe still hadn't returned Faith's call—but Faith knew they loved her, deep down.

Even if she'd like them to show it a little differently.

Had God put the Santos family in her life, too? That might be a stretch, considering she and Tom were competing for the same building. There were blessings even in that struggle, though. The kids were funny, bright and sweet, and being around them made her smile.

Tom made her smile, too, but that was definitely not something she wanted to think about.

Bettina meowed, dragging Faith's attention to the present. "Yes, I thank God for you, too. Do you want to go back to sleep, purr-ball?"

In answer, Bettina tucked her nose beneath a paw.

Her spirits lighter, Faith freshened up, changing into clean jeans, a floral blouse and ballerina flats. The store didn't close for another twenty minutes, so she could get some things done before Angie left. She'd stepped onto the staircase landing when her cell phone buzzed in her jeans pocket.

Faith didn't recognize the number, but it was local. "Hello?"

"Faith? It's Jason Witt from Sparky's."

The electrician she'd talked to about fixing up the mid-century desk. "Hi, Jason. How are you?"

"I had a cancelation, and I wondered if this would be a good time for me to look at that desk you told me about."

"Perfect time. But be careful driving in. The old schoolhouse burned down this afternoon, and Main Street is closed off at the south end."

"I'll take care, then. See you in a few."

It wasn't ten minutes before Jason, a tall young man with a scruffy red-blond beard, entered the antiques store. After he waved at Angie, Faith led him directly to the desk in question. The blond piece had a few dings and needed some work whether or not they altered it to accommodate plugs.

Jason's brown eyes squinted as he gave it the once-over, pulling out drawers and inspecting the backside. At last, he stood up and brushed his hands on his jeans. "The work will be a cinch. We've just got to make sure we don't detract from the integrity of the piece."

Absolutely. "I want it to still look like a mid-century period desk, but at the same time, feel updated, if that makes sense. I'm going to change the knobs out, for one thing." They could definitely use an upgrade.

Jason scratched his ginger-blond beard. "You'll want to do this with other pieces, you said?"

"If this one sells to the hotel, then yes, I'd like to try." She cleared her throat. "What do you think the work will cost?"

"It's a few hours of labor, and the parts won't cost that much." Jason quoted a reasonable price. "It might be something you can do yourself, if you want me to teach you."

"Oh, no." Faith waved her hands. "The work needs to be done by a certified electrician."

"Miss Faith!" Nora's high-pitched voice drew Faith around.

What were Tom and the kids doing here? Nora plowed into her, and Logan crept closer, eyeing Jason with a wary expression. She reached out, and he rushed to her side, hiding his face from Jason. The kids under her arms made her heart feel like exploding with joy.

But it was Tom's small smile that made her stomach swoop low. She looked away from him, fast, to make the introductions.

"Where's Bettina?" Logan pulled back to gaze up at Faith.

"Let Miss Faith finish up her business, son." Tom's reprimand was gentle.

Jason rocked on his heels. "I think we're finished anyway, unless you can think of something else, Faith?"

"Just wondering if I should bring the desk to you?" She'd have to borrow a truck from someone. Who, she couldn't fathom, because her brain had stopped functioning properly when Tom entered the store.

Jason shook his head. "If you've got a work area in that back room, I can do it there. I have a hole in my schedule on Monday."

"That would be fantastic."

As Jason took his exit, Angie grabbed her purse. Looked like she'd swiped on some lipstick since Faith last looked over at her, and she'd also donned a sparkly gemstone statement necklace. "Is it still okay if I go now?"

Ah, yes. Angie's date. "Of course. Have fun."

"Tell Ender hi," Tom said, smiling.

Angie waved, although her parting glance for Faith was quizzical. *What's he doing here?*

Faith shrugged. They'd said goodbyes earlier. As far as she knew, Tom and the kids planned to go home and—

Have pizza and veggies. They'd invited her. And she'd never said no, and neither had Tom. He was too polite to "forget" the kids' invitation.

Tom shoved his hands in the front pockets of his jeans. "With everything that happened with the schoolhouse, we forgot that we'd talked about pizza. We didn't want to leave you hanging, so we thought maybe we should see if you wanted to eat at DeLuca's."

The best pizza in town and right across the street. She should say no for a million reasons. She had to close up the store, she needed distance from Tom so her feelings didn't grow past this insane attraction—

But a girl had to eat. And the kids looked so cute.

One more time, hanging out with them. Just one.

Going out didn't sound appealing, though. The hike, the schoolhouse and overhearing those women in the yarn store had her yearning for a quiet evening. "What do you think about eating here, in my apartment? I still have to close up the store, but if we order the pizza for take-out, it should be ready by the time I'm finished. I have veggies, too."

Tom grinned wide enough to show his pretty-much-perfect teeth. "Deal."

Nora was already on the bottom step to Faith's apartment. "Daddy, don't forget to ask Miss Faith what she likes on her pizza."

Tom adopted a chastised-but-amused expression. "What do you like on your pizza, Faith?"

"Hey, kids, wait for me, if you don't mind." She glanced back at Tom. "Whatever you guys like."

"Pepperoni okay?"

"Perfect."

"I'll head over there now and bring it back. Kids?"

"They can stay with me. Come up through my apartment door, between the store and Apple a Day. I'll leave it unlocked for you."

Tom whistled as he left, and Faith hurried to lock up, deal with the register and clean up the paper coffee cup someone had left on one of the tables. Thankfully, it hadn't left a ring, but Faith polished it up anyway. She dumped the tea from the urn and deemed everything else capable of waiting until tomorrow or Monday morning. "Okay, let's go see Bettina."

The kids ducked beneath the gold cord and ran up the stairs, their feet pounding as if they were in a loudness contest. Logan stopped on the landing, looking at the two doors: one which led to the staircase down to the street door and the other which led to her apartment.

She tipped her head toward the more polished of the two. "That's the one you want. Go on in, it's unlocked."

They ran inside, wide eyes taking in her small but functional kitchen. "Hey, there's our card."

"Of course." The kids' thank-you note was her lone piece of refrigerator art. "Looking at it makes me happy."

"Daddy likes our art, too." Nora led Logan out to the living room, where she touched every piece of furniture, a mix of antiques and newer pieces. Logan pointed down the hallway. "Is that your bedroom?"

"Yep. Bathroom down there, too."

He didn't explore it, captivated instead by the French doors facing east. "This is the balcony we see from outside?"

"Sure is." She took the kids out, showing them the view of Main Street. Then they came back in to find Bettina while Faith unlocked the street door for Tom, washed up and set out some veggies and ranch dip. While the kids and cat played with a string toy, Faith set four places of silverware at the table, something she hadn't done in she couldn't remember how long.

She'd have to do better about inviting people over from now on. She'd focused so long on the museum that she hadn't paid any attention to being social. She hadn't realized how lonely she'd grown.

Ten minutes or so later, she heard the thumping of steps on the private stairwell and the scrape of the door opening onto her landing. Tom and the pizza. Her stomach got jittery, and it had nothing to do with being hungry for pizza.

Although it—they—smelled wonderful. Tom carried in two flat boxes. "One pepperoni and one DeLuca's special. Couldn't resist."

"Perfect. Set them on the counter by the plates. I can't fit them both on the table. I'll get drinks while you guys wash up."

Within five minutes, she'd cut lemon wedges for their water glasses. They clustered in the kitchen, helping the kids select pieces of pizza. They carried them to the table, where the kids paused, as if unsure where to sit. Faith smiled to set them at ease. "Anywhere you like. Shall we sit and say grace?"

She set her pizza down on the nearest toile placemat and then reached to pull out her chair. But Tom's hand was faster. And hers landed right on top of it.

Tom was only trying to pull out her chair, be a gentleman. But when Faith yanked her hand off his, he felt—weirdly disappointed. And not because she pulled her own chair out, denying him the chance to be gallant.

Nora had pizza in her mouth, but she talked anyway. "A girl in my class had a pizza date with her daddy. Now I can say I had a date, too."

"This isn't a daddy-daughter date, honey, and chew with your mouth closed." Tom winked. "This is just friends having dinner."

Faith picked up her pizza. "Maybe you and your daddy can have a pizza date soon, Nora."

"And I can have one with you." Logan smiled shyly at Faith.

"We're good buddies, aren't we?" She nudged his shoulder but didn't make any promises to Tom's relief. Maybe his mom was right about fearing the kids might get attached to Faith. But was that so bad?

She'd be their neighbor, once he was granted the building next door. She was also good to them, kind and loving. His kids needed attachments to adults other than himself, right? His folks, their teachers, his friends like Ender. They needed role models. Faith was a great one—intelligent, industrious and righteous. Why wouldn't he want Nora and Logan to be around her?

"Do you ever have pizza dates, Miss Faith?" Nora took another bite.

"Well, sure, I guess."

"With boys?" Nora talked around her food again.

"Sometimes."

Like whom? Kellan? They'd seemed pretty friendly, sharing that half hug. They probably weren't dating already, or he'd have heard something about it. But they clearly shared a friendship. Their cats came from the same litter. Was a relationship in their future?

Tom washed down his latest bite with a swig of his lemon-infused ice water, chilling him all the way down. It was none of his business, and it wasn't like he was going to date her, either.

At least he could completely refute his mom's concern that Faith was interested in Tom. She was unfazed by the kids' questions, dipping her baby carrots and celery sticks in ranch dressing while conversing as if she hadn't a care in the world.

Finished, Logan wiped his hands on a napkin. "Do you have any games?"

"Board games?" Faith's brows knit. "Do you want to play something?"

"Not if you're busy, Faith." They'd imposed long enough.

"No, it sounds fun. I don't have a lot of games, but I have something down in the store that I could bring up."

Nora wiggled on her chair. "An old game?"

"From the fifties, yes. I've been curious what it's like, and it's not in pristine condition so our playing it won't hurt anything. Besides, if we play, I can tell a prospective buyer what it's like. Unless it's so fun I want to keep it all to myself."

Tom glanced at the pizza crusts on the kids' plates. "The kids and I will clear up while you go get it."

While Faith ran downstairs, Tom helped the kids toss food scraps into the trash before he put the plates into the dishwasher. Before he could put the remaining pizza in the fridge, Faith was back with a pale green box that was worn at the corners. Dampening the dishrag, Tom swiped crumbs from the table so they could set the game on it.

"I could get used to this," Faith teased.

"A cleanup crew?" Surely, she didn't mean him and the kids being around.

She didn't answer but laughed and opened the box.

Within a few minutes, the kids were fully engaged in the shopping-themed game, even as Faith had to explain to them what some of the old-timey sounding stores on the board were. "A haberdasher was a hat store."

"Haberdasher sounds funny." Logan snickered.

Nora couldn't repeat the word, for giggling. "Haber-dishy."

It was silly, but his kids' silliness was precious to Tom. Their wide-mouth laughs revealed budding teeth in places where the baby teeth had come out. In a year, they'd look totally different, so he memorized the smiles around the table.

Even Faith's. They could never be more than friends, but he couldn't deny that he liked looking at her grin.

He also liked that she found his kids funny when they got a bad case of the sillies. Not everyone could take their six-year-old humor for long.

"Haber-ducky." Nora snorted.

"Haber-shusher," Logan added, making Nora roar.

"You guys are something," Tom said, moving his metal game piece. It made a soft thunk on the cardstock board. But the noise didn't stop when he took his hand off the figure.

Thunk, thunk, thunk.

Faith's eyes grew large. "That's my private door from the street. I forgot to lock it after you came in."

Tom leaped to his feet. "You're not expecting any-one?"

Her head shook.

It could be a neighbor, or a curious tourist poking around…or something far more sinister. Pizza and anx-iety churning in his stomach, Tom dashed to her front door. "I'll take care of it, but have your phone ready just in case."

In case we need to call the police. Her nod said she understood.

Out on the landing, he swung open the door to the staircase he'd come up with the pizza, his hands fisting with tension. Who would he encounter? Confused visitors, robbers, what?

He didn't expect a blonde woman carrying a duffel bag two stairs down.

"Chloe?" Faith's confused voice sailed past him from the landing.

Tom's shoulders sagged in relief. Faith's sister, and sure enough, she looked just as he remembered, with her blond curls, green eyes and preference to dress in bright, trendy clothing. Faith would be so glad to see her—

Chloe wrapped her arms around Tom's neck. "Tomás Santos, what are you doing here?"

"Pizza and a board game." Tom extricated himself quickly. Great as it was to see Chloe, he didn't want to get in the way of her seeing Faith. "What about you?"

"Answering an SOS call." Chloe tucked a blond curl behind her ear. "I hear you're competing with Faith for the stinky old store next door."

"It's not stinky. It's got character."

"Yeah, yeah," she teased. "We clearly have a lot to catch up on."

"I'll take your bag." Tom reached for her suitcase.

When he looked up to the door to smile at Faith, she was gone.

Chapter Eleven

Chloe was here. Unannounced, unexpected, but in response to Faith's call. Faith should feel happy, but the only thing she felt was her dinner sitting in a lump in her stomach. Watching Chloe wrap her arms around Tom's neck hadn't been fun. In fact, Faith might not even have been present, for all the attention Chloe gave her before Tom and the kids left to go home a few minutes ago.

Since then, Chloe had been on her phone, tapping away, although she'd followed Faith into the guest room. Faith tugged a clean fitted sheet over the mattress harder than necessary. "This is a surprise, seeing you."

"You called me, remember?"

You didn't answer, remember? "That was like, ten days ago." Faith unfurled the top sheet over the bed.

Chloe pocketed her phone and yanked the sheet so hard the opposite corner flew out of Faith's hands. "I was waiting to find out if I could get time off work before I made a promise I couldn't keep."

Faith had never asked for her sister to come for a visit. She'd just asked for a five-minute conversation where her sister said *there, there* or *I'm sorry.*

Instead, Chloe gave her something more than she'd ever considered receiving from her sister. The support of her presence. And for that, she should be grateful.

"You didn't have to do that," she said quietly. "But I really appreciate it."

"Don't get all sentimental, Faith, but it's been on my mind lately that I'm not always the best sister. Nothing set me off, nothing happened, but I've been thinking about you."

"I've been thinking about you, too." Praying, actually. Was this God's answer?

Chloe tucked in her side of the sheet, then helped tug the fuzzy cream blanket and red toile bedspread back atop the bed. "I figured you didn't need me or anything, but my guess is that Mom and Dad weren't that helpful when you told them."

"I didn't tell them. They're both traveling, and I didn't want to bug them."

"They might not have understood, anyway. They've never been supportive of the store and probably don't think the museum is a profitable idea."

"True." Mom and Dad might be divorced, but they had plenty of similar opinions when it came to Faith's life choices. "They don't understand this is what I want to do, even if it doesn't lead to wealth."

"Or why you want to be in Widow's Peak Creek. They hated it here. The only reason they stayed so long was Dad's admin job at the hospital. He'd been searching for a new job for years."

Faith looked up from smoothing the pillows. "I didn't know any of that."

"I overheard them talk about it several times, but I never told you. I knew you'd freak out."

Despite all of her parents' arguments, she'd nevertheless been devastated by the divorce and their move away, so yeah. She would have.

Faith slipped out to the hall cupboard and returned with a beige terry towel and washcloth. "I'm relieved they're traveling, in all honestly. If I tell them I might not get the museum, I'm afraid they'll tell me it's a sign to move away and do something else with my life."

Like work at a fancy auction house, like Dad thought she should do. Or teach, like Mom wanted.

Chloe came around to Faith's side of the bed. "Look, I know I don't totally get the museum thing, and I'm not good at keeping in touch, but I'll be there to support you at the council meeting on Tuesday." Moving words that made Faith teary, but Chloe was not an emotional person. Instead, she wiggled her expertly-plucked eyebrows. "If you still need my support, that is. I expected you and Tom Santos to be at each other's throats. Instead, the enemy was here tonight, having pizza."

"He's not the enemy. We're rivals for the same piece of real estate but it's important to both of us that we handle the conflict well." She explained how Tom's kids overheard their argument. "So we're kind of trying to be friends, I guess."

"That stinks."

"That we had a big fight in front of his kids?"

"No, that you're stuck in the friend zone with Tom Santos. I sure wouldn't want to be."

"You're interested in Tom?" Faith's stomach pinched as she recalled how Chloe had practically lunged into Tom's arms on the stairwell.

"Of course not. I haven't talked to him in eons." Chloe waved away the suggestion. "It was fun seeing him again tonight, though. Catching up on the past. I would think you'd approve of us revisiting history."

"High school history isn't my favorite." Being an awkward ugly duckling, their parents' divorce, moving away—not a lot of good memories, as she and Chloe had just touched on. "I'd better get to bed, but I leave for church at 9:15 if you want to come."

"Sure." Chloe yawned, wide and loud like a cartoon character. "Where's the outlet in here? These creaky old buildings never have enough of them."

After pointing out the outlet by the door—an odd spot, but who knows what the thinking had been for it once upon a time—Faith quickly told her about Tom's idea for her to refurbish furniture. "Maybe I should fix up something to go in here, too. Next time you visit, you can plug your devices into the nightstand, maybe."

"Ooh, that'll be helpful. But I thought you wanted to preserve old things."

"Sometimes preservation may need a boost. This desk I'm fixing up? It needs help, anyway. I've got the cutest green drawer knobs, art deco, but the effect on the mid-century desk is going to give it a fun vibe I think Willa at the Cordova will like." Faith stopped, sure she was boring her sister. Chloe had come to help her out, but this topic wasn't her thing, so Faith just smiled. Chloe didn't have to get it. She was here, and that was a start. "I'll let you rest."

Chloe blew her a kiss. "Night, night."

No big hug. No display of emotion like she'd given Tom, but that was okay. Her sister was here for her, no other reason. "Thanks for coming, Chloe. Really."

"Sure thing. Hey, do you have good coffee in the kitchen? Or awful stuff?"

After establishing Faith's coffee supply would pass muster, Faith showered and crawled into bed. Bettina curled at her feet. As long and overwhelming as the day had been, Faith expected to crash immediately, but she had a hard time falling asleep. The day replayed in her head like an old VHS tape, rewinding back to key events, all of which involved Tom.

Him shutting her car door for her. His hands on her shoulders. His gaze on her lips.

She rolled over and punched the pillow. *You're reading too much into things, Latham. And even if you weren't, what would you want? Another relationship with someone who thought you were more outdated than his grandma? Someone who thought the same about her and her museum idea as those women in town today but at least was nicer about it?*

Faith wasn't stuck in the past. She had nothing against technology. She didn't value antiques because of their financial worth. She appreciated them because of the stories they could tell, for what they taught about how people once lived. And things, like people, didn't need to be tossed aside when something flashier or sleeker came along.

The way her parents seemed to have done with each other. The way Chloe went through car leases. The way Faith's one and only relationship had gone south when he grew bored with Widow's Peak Creek, her antiquing and, yeah, her.

Better to focus instead on God's blessings today. Daffodils. The kids' giggles. Chloe driving here from the Bay Area to support her. She'd have liked some warning, but she wanted to improve her relationship with her sister, didn't she?

It's the principle of the matter. Chloe actually came.

The next morning, Chloe actually made it to church, too, despite sleeping until Faith was sure she'd have to go alone. They slunk into the back row just after the service had started.

Nora and Logan, seated up front with their dad and grandparents, turned around as if looking for someone. When they saw her, they waved, grinning.

Faith waved back.

Tom peeked over his shoulder and smiled at her. She shoved away the little thrill his smile gave her.

She forced her attention to fix on the Scriptures and sermon after that—a timely topic, loving your neighbor—until the final notes of the closing hymn. Logan was on her before she could stuff her bulletin into her purse.

"Miss Faith." His little arms wrapped around her waist.

"Hi, handsome." She hugged back. "Hi, pretty." She reached out for Nora.

The sweetness of their return hugs was cut short by Tom's parents catching up to the kids, leaving Tom lagging behind in conversation with an elder. Though Roberto's black hair was streaked with gray and his tan skin wrinkled around the eyes and mouth, he looked so much like Tom up close that Faith could easily imagine what Tom would look like in a few decades. Minus the mustache, of course.

"Good morning." Faith smiled at Tom's frowning parents. "This is my sister, Chloe."

As they exchanged polite greetings, Nora stepped away from Faith, but Logan stayed put beneath the shelter of Faith's arm. Little snuggle bug.

Until Elena snatched Logan's hand and pulled him away from Faith.

Wow, they didn't much want to socialize with her, did they? They must be terribly upset she was competing against Tom for the building.

She understood their reasons, but she and Tom had resolved to rise above it. As Tom approached, Faith was determined to try to set a better example for the kids. "Hi, Tom."

"Hey. Folks, did you meet Faith's sister, Chloe Latham? We were at school together."

"Just now." Elena smiled the same way she did on her real-estate flyers, a smile she'd yet to bestow on Faith.

Chloe jerked her thumb at Tom and then Faith. "Tuesday's a big day for these two, right? Duking it out at city council."

It was a joke, but Roberto and Elena didn't even twitch their lips. Elena laid a possessive hand on Logan's head. "I don't think it will be much of a contest. No offense, Faith, but a museum won't bring in tax revenue the way an exciting new store will."

How was she not supposed to be offended by that? Faith forced herself to remember that Elena was trying to protect her son.

"Actually," Tom said, looking at her, "this town needs a museum. Just like it will benefit from an outdoor gear store. Faith and I are in perfect agreement about that. We disagree about where the museum and store should each be, that's all. But like the sermon reminded us, loving your neighbor isn't always smooth."

Could he read her thanks in her eyes? She read something in his—not words, exactly, but warmth.

Logan patted her arm. "We're going out for Mexican food now. You could come with us."

"Yeah, come." Nora jumped, making her pink dahlia-print dress swish.

"Not this time. I'm going to have lunch with my sister, and you're going to have fun with your grandparents." It seemed best in every way. Tom's parents didn't much like her, and Faith wouldn't be in danger of falling deeper into this unwanted attraction she had for Tom. Win-win, all the way around.

A few more minutes of small talk and Faith jingled her car keys, a signal as old as the automobile. "Ready, Chloe?"

"Sure." They said goodbye to the Santos clan. On the way out to the parking lot, Chloe gripped Faith's arm. "Mexican food sounds really good for lunch, though. I could go for some nachos. I wish you'd have said yes."

"I'll make us nachos for lunch."

"They won't be as good as the ones from the restaurant."

"Probably not." Story of her life, when it came to her family.

But she'd make her sister nachos anyway, and then she'd get to work preparing for her presentation to city council on Tuesday. It was time to focus on the future she'd long hoped for. She would be ready.

The next morning over coffee with Ender, Tom leaned back in his chair at Angel Food Bakery and his stretch cracked his back.

Ender grimaced at the sound. "Yikes."

"Sorry, I was hunched over my computer until late last night, looking over my proposal for tomorrow's meeting."

"Is it finished?" Ender lifted his paper coffee cup to his lips.

Tom tipped one ear down toward one shoulder, stretching his neck. "Yeah, but I'll look it over once more tonight."

"Why so glum? You worried about losing the storefront to Faith?"

"Not exactly." The mayor was in his corner. Other folks seemed to want his store on Main Street, too.

"Cheer up, then. You're going to get everything you want. And you can finally put me on the payroll. Don't get me wrong, I'm grateful for the job at the auto-parts store, but I'm ready to work for you."

"Believe me, I am so grateful for your help, Ender. You've got experience with both retail and camping gear, which I sorely lack." Tom would hopefully make up for it with his exuberance and determination, as well as what he'd learned in his last few years of work. "This…situation with Faith is odd, that's all. Two good things competing for space."

"I'm kind of surprised you support a museum now. You never struck me as the history type."

"Faith's opened my eyes to that, I guess." He swallowed his last bite of bear claw pastry, savoring the almond sweetness.

"You're sure nothing else is going on with you and Faith? And by else, I mean, you know, you liking her?"

"Nope."

"I admire your devotion to your kids. You've totally turned your life around, and that's good. I want to support you any way I can. That's the only reason I ask, because you told me how sold you were on your parents' idea that you not date. Just want to make sure you're not struggling with that."

"Faith is a likable person. But that's it. I'm not in love with her or anything." Tom crumpled his napkin, signaling a definite change in topic. "Hey, do you know anything about a men's Bible study group at Del's Café on Wednesday mornings? Early breakfast, that sort of thing."

"No, I haven't heard of it, but I'd go. How'd you find out?"

"Kellan at the bookstore. Sounds like all are welcome." Tom hadn't been in a small group since leaving San Francisco, and gathering with fellow men to study Scripture sounded helpful. Except for one thing. "Do you know anything about him?"

"The bookstore guy?"

"Kellan, yeah."

"I'm not a big reader so I don't go in his store much. Why?"

"No reason." He couldn't admit the guy's friendship with Faith made him the teeniest bit jealous. He had no right. "We'd better get going. I don't want to make you late."

Ender glanced at his wristwatch. "I have enough time to drop into the antiques store to say hi to Angie first."

"I'm heading that way. I'm going to peek in the livery window one last time before tomorrow's big presentation."

It wasn't yet ten in the morning, so there weren't many cars parked in front of the Main Street shops. But there was a large white van emblazoned with the Sparky's Electric logo. "You know, I'll pop in with you. I want to see how Jason's doing with the desk he's retrofitting for Faith."

Faith had already set up her outdoor display, the green chairs and table with the basket of drawer knobs. On the chalkboard, she'd written, *Antiques shopping is my cardio. Heart-quickening finds inside!*

Though the closed sign hung in the door, Angie saw them through the window and unlocked the door. "Hey, you two."

Tom's greeting for Angie was short and sweet. She was more interested in Ender, anyway. Faith looked up, surprise shining in her eyes. "Tom, I'm glad you could see this."

"Yeah?"

"It's all done. I'm texting pictures to Willa at the Cordova, to see what she thinks."

Tom bent to examine the work Faith and Jason had done, the discreet outlet insert on the desktop plus the addition of a cord clamp on the back to give a tidy look to whatever electronic devices the hotel might place atop the desk. Faith had polished the desk to a gleaming shine and affixed funky green drawer knobs. It was functional and, no other word for it, cool. "She'll love it."

"I hope so." Faith grinned. It was fun to see her so happy.

"I'm heading out," Ender called. "See you all later."

"I should go, as well." Jason patted the desk.

"Everyone leaves just as I'm coming downstairs." Dressed in a peacock-colored quilted jacket and matching beanie, Chloe let herself through the gold cord, carrying with her the strong floral fragrance of just-applied cologne.

"Good morning." Faith gestured at the tea cart. "Want some hot tea?"

"Tea? Blech. I'm going to run to the bakery for a double espresso."

"How about you, Tom?" Faith tucked her hair behind her ear, drawing his attention to her graceful neck. The coloring of her apricot and green floral blouse was a perfect complement to her skin tone. She always dressed in a flattering, classic way, though. Like she knew what suited her.

Tom shoved his hands in his pockets, suddenly feeling shy. Bizarre—he hadn't been shy since…ever? "No, thanks. I just had a cup of coffee but I wanted to stop in and see the desk."

"That's really nice of you, Tom." Faith's smile warmed him inside out, better than the coffee had.

Chloe glanced at the desk but didn't linger. "I've gotta say, I'm on Team Faith for obvious reasons, but you guys are handling this competition better than I'd expected. Or maybe I'm missing it because I am in such dire need of coffee. See you in a few."

"I'd better go, as well," he told Faith, as Chloe left. "I need groceries. It's a lot easier to handle that particular chore without the kids."

"They're eager to help you buy things you don't need, I'm guessing." She followed him toward the door, then out of it so they were standing on the concrete by her green chairs.

"Nora begs, but Logan's sneaky. I didn't even notice him hiding Danishes in the cart last time until we were checking out. Gum, too. And that candy that looks like a giant ring."

She laughed. "You're off your game, Tom."

"I'm overwhelmed, is what I am." But he laughed with her. "Parenting isn't for wimps."

"I imagine not. But you're doing a great job."

"Yeah?"

"Your kids are fabulous. Sneaky, maybe, but I'm quite fond of them. I'm glad they helped us get over our…antagonism? Is that a good word?"

"You sorta hated me."

"I never hated you. But you definitely underestimated me."

"I did," Tom agreed. "I was wrong. You're a force, Faith Latham."

"I'd say the same about you, Tomás Santos."

No one called him Tomás anymore, except his parents. When he went to college, he'd wanted to start fresh, so he'd introduced himself as Tom.

But his full name sounded like honey from Faith's lips.

A buzzing sound jolted him from the crazy direction of his thoughts and made Faith break eye contact. She tugged her phone from her pocket and her lips parted. "It's Willa. She loves the desk."

"Of course she does. Faith, that's wonderful."

He had never seen Faith wear such a look of delighted astonishment, her lips parted in a sweet smile, her eyes blinking as if she didn't believe what she'd read. "She's paying full asking price. I tried to be fair, but I expected there to be negotiation."

"I'm sure your pricing was more than fair, Faith."

"She loved the knobs." Faith squeaked, the way Nora did when she was excited. "And she wants more furnishings. This is going to get the store through its off-season slump, Tom. I can't believe it. And it's thanks to you."

"I didn't do anything. That was you. And Jason from Sparky's."

"It was *your idea*." Faith mock-punched his bicep.

"I had no idea if it would work. You're the one who went with it."

"Oh, Tom, I'm so happy right now."

Tom couldn't help it. He pulled her into his arms and whirled her in a circle. Two circles. He lost the ability to count the moment she was close to him, laughing in his ear. He didn't want to let her go, but he had to, for propriety's sake, if nothing else.

Feet back on the ground, she grinned up at him. "We've come a long way, haven't we?"

"I'd say so."

"You ready for tomorrow?"

"I think so. Should I wear a tie?"

"Probably." Her gaze dropped to his throat, where the necktie knot would be. "And shave."

"What's wrong with my scruff?"

"Not a thing." Her cheeks pinked. "I just thought men shaved for important events."

"Sometimes, I guess." He scratched his chin. "Your presentation finished?"

"Yep, and Chloe's having dinner with friends so I have all evening to practice."

"You shouldn't be alone tonight."

"No?"

He shook his head. "You'll get nervous. Come to dinner tonight. Roscoe and the kids will distract you."

Her mouth twisted. "Are you serving Danishes and candy rings?"

"You'll have to come to find out."

She looked at the concrete beneath her feet for a second. "Okay."

"Okay?" He'd expected an argument.

"You're right. I'll fret if I'm home alone. So what should I bring?"

"Just yourself. Come after you close the store."

"Okay." She walked backward. "Thanks, Tom. It's a nice thing you're doing for me."

He hoped so, but there was a lot of selfishness in his invitation, too. He wanted to be with her one more time before the city council presentations.

Because tomorrow, everything would change. Only one of them would get the old livery. If Faith received permission to turn it into her museum, Tom would be happy for her, but he'd be frustrated, too. He needed that building so he could be on Main Street for the sake of his twins.

If he received permission to start his store on Main Street, she'd be happy for him, too, wouldn't she? And just as frustrated that she lost?

What would that look like in their relationship?

They'd stay civil, sure, but tomorrow, no matter how things turned out at the council meeting, their friendship might be dealt a fatal blow.

The idea carved a hole in his gut.

Chapter Twelve

Faith rubbed her full stomach. It was a good thing they were heading out back for a post-dinner walk along the creek, because she needed to work off some of the garlic bread and spaghetti Tom had prepared before dessert. "I've never had Danishes for dessert, but I'm excited. I've been thinking about them all day, since you mentioned them earlier."

As they made their way to the sliding glass door to the backyard, Nora tapped the plate of plastic-wrapped pastries with dollops of jewel-bright jellies in their centers. "When we come back from our walk, you can choose between raspberry, apricot and cherry."

"Apricot, definitely." Faith's favorite.

Tom met Faith's gaze as he donned a green down vest over his plaid shirt, a color that made his already-dark eyes deepen to ink. "Do you want a jacket?"

Earlier this afternoon, temperatures had dipped, so after work Faith had changed into a bronze-colored turtleneck and jeans. The creamy scarf she'd wrapped around her shoulders added an extra layer of warmth. "I'm fine."

Tom clipped Roscoe's leash to his collar and led them out the sliding back door. The spring evening smelled of young leaves, fresh grass and musky flowering pear blossoms. Tom's cologne laced the air, too, which had to be the absolute best thing on the market, whatever it was.

No, Latham, she chastised herself as if she were giving Roscoe a talking to.

The kids had already run across the yard and pulled on the locked gate. "Can we walk to the big boulder?" Logan pointed to the right.

"Not tonight. Too far." Tom glanced back at Faith. "I don't want them out at the creek unsupervised, so I have to lock the gate."

Faith had wandered the creek alone plenty in her childhood, and Widow's Peak Creek was a quiet town, but times had changed. Besides, Tom had other reasons for keeping close watch on his children. "Safety first. I get it."

"I can be paranoid when it comes to the kids." He rolled his eyes at himself before unlocking the latch and letting the kids free.

"I wouldn't use that word. I'd say responsible," she countered.

"Ender says I need to trust God more."

"We all do, but that doesn't mean you should let your kids play near the creek without an adult. They're six, Tom."

"Yeah, you're right."

Faith breathed deeply of the sweet evening air as they walked on the dirt path along the creek. "This is wonderful. The sun hasn't gone down yet, the creek is bubbling, the birds are singing."

"The kids are yelling loud enough to bug the neighborhood," he continued in imitation of her sing-song tone.

She laughed. "They're happy. So's Roscoe."

The dog pattered just ahead of them on the leash, wagging his thick tail.

"I was worried the kids would have trouble adjusting to our move, but they're doing great so far."

"Prayer helps, and I'm sure you've been doing a lot of that."

"I have. That and focusing on them and the store. This is the extent of my social life, beyond coffee with Ender."

"Well, we need to do something about that, then."

The minute she said it, anxiety gripped her chest. Did that sound like she was fishing? Like she wanted to go on a date with him? Because she didn't.

Actually, she did. She wanted him to pick her up and twirl her around like he had earlier today, leaving her breathless and giddy.

But she was not fishing. And she and Tom were not a good pair. They were competitors. In completely different places in life. They wanted different things. So she shrugged like the matter was trivial. "You and Ender, I mean."

His silence surprised her enough that she looked back at him. His gaze was fixed on the ground ahead of them, like he watched his kids' feet. "Yeah, the whole lack of a social life thing has been on purpose."

"Sure. Grieving is—well, I can't imagine what the three of you have gone through." The loss of her grandparents was like a wound that was sometimes still tender to touch. But Tom's loss? How much worse must it be? "I'm sure you miss your wife terribly."

"Of course. Lourdes will always be a part of me and the kids. But grief changes, you know?"

"Yeah." Thinking of her grandparents didn't sting in quite the same way anymore.

"I just don't want to leave the kids at all, and if I did, my parents would hound me about it. They're convinced I'll ignore the kids because I wasn't around much in San Francisco, even though Lourdes wanted me to work the way I did. I feel like they're waiting for the other shoe to drop."

That didn't seem very supportive of his parents. "You're a great dad, Tom. Everyone can see that. Dredging up the past like that can't be helpful."

"I get it, though. I get it like a punch in the gut with each new milestone the kids reach, because I wasn't around for the earlier ones. They're losing teeth now. I was at a conference when they got teeth as babies. They're getting ready for me to take the training wheels off their bikes, but I missed them riding tricycles. I can never forget it, never forgive myself for not being there. But my parents want to ensure I don't forget, either. Even though I promised them my life would be nothing but the kids and a balanced work life—no relationships, no nothing—they don't seem to believe me."

No relationships.

Well, at least now she could confirm—to herself, when she was weak, thinking about Tom—that they were solidly in the friend zone, which was best for everyone. Even though it felt like two factions of emotion warred each other within her rib cage. Relief, because her attraction to Tom was fruitless and she hadn't wanted to be in a relationship anyway. But also grief, because part of her shouted that her feelings went beyond attraction. She was in danger of falling in love with the guy—

Step back from that pool of quicksand, Latham. Being in danger of something isn't the same as actually being in it. You still have a chance to save yourself.

Since they were friends, though, she would try to be a good one. "You're a great dad, Tom. I've seen it. Is it possible your parents are overreacting?"

"Maybe, but I don't want to blow it again, Faith."

"You won't blow it."

"I chose work over my family before. I'm capable of doing it again. And once the store gets up and running? What if I get lost in work again, like I did before Lourdes died?"

"You're not the same person you were a year ago. Six months ago, even. That's the work of God in you, and you doing all you can to set your priorities right."

His dark eyes met hers, blazing in their intensity. Oh, no, here she went again, weak-kneed and jittery.

"You're right, Faith. Thank you."

She wanted to say something pithy and funny to lighten the moment. Instead, all she could manage was, "You're welcome."

Slick.

Nora yelled back at them. "Can we cross the bridge?"

They'd stopped at one of the footbridges connecting neighborhoods on either side of the creek. It was a charming picture-taking spot for kids going to prom and family photos, a place to capture memories.

Faith may not have a camera, but she'd never forget this moment, both kids looking back at her and their dad, their sweet faces eager.

"Sure, just don't lean over the side," Tom called,

watching the kids but not hurrying to join them. They took their time getting to the bridge, letting the kids run over it several times before they crossed it with Roscoe to the other side of the creek. A wide path between two backyards opened to a neighborhood street, and Tom glanced at his watch. "Five minutes over here and then we should probably walk back."

"Aww," Logan groaned.

"It's a school night. Plus, there are Danishes waiting at home."

"And you and I have a big day tomorrow, too," she reminded Tom. Early bed wouldn't be a bad idea. "Thanks for inviting me over as a distraction."

"Did it work?"

"It did. I haven't thought of my presentation at all tonight. Or Chloe leaving on Wednesday."

"Have you two had a good visit?"

"Better than I expected. We're still very different, but she's here, you know? It's an answer to prayer." Evidence of God working on her relationship with her sister. She mustn't lose sight of that.

Nor should she lose sight of the other blessings this rivalry had brought, like her strange friendship with Tom and the kids. And the fact that she'd decided to trust God for the outcome, which filled her anew with an inexplicable peace. "You're going to do great tomorrow at city council."

"So will you." Tom beckoned the kids to turn back with them. "I'm going to pray we both sleep well tonight and do our best."

"I like that, Tom. Thanks."

It was yet one more thing to add to the list of things to like about Tom Santos.

What number am I on, Lord? A hundred and twelve?
The smile he gave her was definitely number two on the
list. Number one was the way he loved his kids, which
made her insides get all squishy when she saw him in-
teract with them. Like it did right now, when he teased
and ran with the kids over the bridge.

Clearly, she wasn't doing very well putting her attraction for him into a box that she could lock up and throw
away the key.

The next morning, however, Faith found yet one more
thing to like about Tom when she spied him outside the
city council building dressed in a gray suit—clean-
shaven. As good as he looked all scruffy, he looked just
as good, if not better, like this.

*What number is that, now, God? A hundred and thir-
teen?*

His admiring glance took in her jade green dress and
cream-colored blazer. "You look nice."

"So do you," she blurted. Understatement of the year.

Chloe caught up to them, carrying the paper cup of
coffee she'd just bought from a street vendor half a block
down. "Hi, Tom. You guys ready to go inside?"

Faith glanced at Chloe's full cup. "They probably
won't let you take your drink in there."

"I'll hurry." She blew on the steaming black brew.

Tom met Faith's gaze. "Are you ready, Faith? Doing
okay?"

What a far cry from where they'd been less than two
weeks ago when he showed up with the mayor to look at
the old livery. "I'm nervous, but yes. The shop is closed
so Angie can be here and I could focus on preparing for
this. But instead of going over my presentation, I've been

praying. For both of us. However this plays out, God will still be in charge, right?"

"Right. And no matter what happens, I hope you and I will still be friends, Faith."

Until that moment, she hadn't realized how awful it would be if they didn't stay friends. She'd miss the kids like crazy. And Roscoe's nudges. And him, of course. A thousand times him.

"I'd like that, Tom."

Tom's parents came up the sidewalk, wearing Sunday-best clothes and smiles, which turned to frowns once they saw her with Tom. She forced a smile. "Good morning, Mr. Santos, Mrs. Santos."

Roberto nodded, but Elena didn't meet Faith's gaze. "Big day. Let's go, Tom. You don't want any distractions right now."

He hesitated like he had something else to say, but then he nodded. "See you inside."

"Bye." Faith wouldn't mind taking her seat anyway, so she could go through her notes. "Are you almost done with your espresso?"

"Close." Chloe took another sip. "Tom may be the enemy, but he looks good in that suit, doesn't he, Faith?"

Thanks to prayer, Faith was calmer than she'd expected to be, but that didn't mean she didn't have any nerves at all—and Chloe's comment had just made them come to life. "I thought you weren't interested in him."

"I'm not, but you are, sure as this espresso is not up to my usual standards."

Faith blinked. "I don't even know what you mean."

"This espresso is awful."

"I meant about Tom."

Chloe rolled her eyes. "You like him, and he likes you."

"Nope." She'd laugh if it weren't so ridiculous.

"Yep." Chloe tossed her half-full cup into the nearest trash can.

"No." Faith had to lower her voice. "For one, I am not interested in another relationship like my last one." Her only real relationship.

"Seriously? You're letting the memory of that lawyer guy you dated keep you from having any sort of life now? What was his name, your old boyfriend? You're still hung up on him?" Chloe led the way up the concrete stairs to the door of city hall.

"Brad." Faith held her sister back so they wouldn't be overheard by half the town. "And of course I'm over him. But that doesn't mean I've forgotten the lesson I learned from him. Brad and I gelled in some ways, but we ultimately valued different things. Well, Tom and I value different things, too. I don't want to be like Mom and Dad, complaining all the time about the other's interests. I want to be with someone who cares about the things I do."

"First of all, Mom and Dad didn't set a good example for us when it comes to relationships. Second, if you're talking about sharing a love of antiques with a man, that'd be great, but I think you're off base. You should look for someone who values God and family and this town. Who cares whether that guy is a nut over gramophones or tintypes? Tom is the sort of person who'd be excited for you when you find something when you're off antiquing. And if he liked baseball or camping, that's not a deal breaker. You'd be happy for him to enjoy his passions even if you don't understand them. You and Tom have differences, but learning about the other has seemed to enrich you, not deplete you."

Faith had to push her emotions down hard before they clogged her throat. "Okay, maybe. A little. But friendship is all there will ever be between us, and you know what? This totally is not the time to discuss it." She strode into the lobby of city hall.

"I brought it up because you were looking at each other like moon-eyed saps."

"We were not. He has no interest in dating. He told me, so can we drop this now?"

Chloe gaped. "Of course we can't. Spill the beans, woman."

Why did they have to do this outside of the council chamber? "He's focused on his kids and nothing else, okay? No relationships. So there's no future."

Only once she said it out loud did she recognize the ache in her stomach that had nothing to do with today's meeting, or the museum or anything related to work.

It was Tom. She did have feelings for him. Not ones she wanted to examine too closely, but…something.

And Chloe was right—Tom was nothing like Brad. Or either of her parents, who disregarded the aspects of Faith's life that didn't interest them. Tom was open to them, and she'd opened up to things in his world, too.

If things were different, she might have wanted to date Tom. But he wasn't available, and she had a choice to make where he was concerned. Friends or nothing.

She chose friends. Hands down.

Fortunately, Chloe couldn't continue to badger her because the wave of folks in suits and pencil skirts heading toward the council chamber crested over them, and they had to go inside. Time to transition back to the moment and not think about Tom. *Museum, museum, museum.*

Faith's stomach buzzed like a hive of nerves. It was

difficult not to look at the horseshoe-shaped desks on a dais where Mayor Hughes and the other members of the city council would sit in mere moments. Or at Tom, who sat beside his parents and Ender in the front row, smiling at her.

His wasn't the only smile, though. Maeve sat near the front of the audience. So did Angie. Even Kellan was here, along with a few other shop owners from Main Street.

"You can do this," Chloe said.

Faith couldn't speak anymore. All she could do was nod and find a seat so she could organize her presentation materials.

This is it, God. If this is Your will, You'll see it done. And if it isn't? I'll need Your help to know what to do next.

She let out a breath and met Tom's gaze as the meeting came to order.

Showtime.

By the time Faith was finished with her presentation, Tom was half-ready to vote for it himself. If he had a vote, that is. She'd laid out the need for a central place for tourists to stop in Widow's Peak Creek, like a museum dedicated to its history. She'd clearly brushed up on her knowledge of funding and revenue issues, sharing statistics from neighboring Gold Country communities. She talked about the town landmarks, from the big boulder to what was left of the Raven Mine, and how the town would benefit from a heritage fund to preserve sites, working in tandem with the museum.

She also described how she'd lay out the museum and

what she'd sell in the gift shop—Tom hadn't thought of that aspect of it at all.

Then she made the topic personal, by noting shopkeepers in attendance and sharing what their stores had originally been when the town was founded, mentioning that she possessed artifacts relating to each one.

She'd done her homework.

But so had he, and he was ready when it was time to stand up.

"I'm from Widow's Peak Creek, and I've decided to make it my home again because it's a special place to raise my children. It's all about family. So is my store, The World Outside. It will carry stock to help bring folks closer together as they explore the natural beauty surrounding us here. There's not a similar store within miles, and my store will not only provide jobs as I hire employees but it will draw visitors to the heart of our historic district, where they'll undoubtedly visit the other establishments."

He spoke for a few more minutes, and when he finished making his case, Ender and his parents grinned at him. He'd done well in their eyes, as well as his own.

But he was most curious about Faith's reaction. He wanted to remain friends. But would it be possible now that they were actually in the moment of decision?

Her smile assured him they were okay, and it was hard not to laugh at her discreet thumbs-up.

The sound of Mayor Hughes stacking papers in front of her drew his attention back to the dais. "I think we've seen enough. Shall we put it to a vote?"

"No discussion?" Tom blinked. He'd expected the decision to take longer. He leaned toward his parents. "It's like they decided before we made our presentations."

"It's not like jury duty." Mom chuckled.

It didn't seem right, though.

"We've done our own research into what spot could occupy the vacant building on Main Street," Mayor Hughes continued, adjusting the fuchsia bow of her blouse tied at her throat. "Based on our understanding of projected tax revenues and so forth, I think we're ready to come to a decision. Does anyone on the council disagree?"

"I move to close discussion and vote," said a man in his midforties seated beside the mayor.

"I so second." A woman—the dentist, maybe—didn't look up from her notes.

"In favor?" Mayor Hughes arched a brow.

"Aye," they all said.

"Let's vote by a show of hands," the mayor said. "All in favor of Mr. Santos renting the vacant property at number one Main Street for his outdoor gear store, please raise your hand."

Every member of the council raised his or her hands. The vote was unanimous.

Mayor Hughes met Tom's gaze. "Congratulations, Mr. Santos, you are hereby granted permission to rent number one Main Street. As you are aware, renting this historic property is both a privilege and a burden. You must comply with the strictures and regulations set forth in…"

The mayor listed codes and lawyer-speak about contracts and duties, but Tom stopped listening. He had the store. The World Outside. Right on the northwest corner of Main Street, the first thing people saw when they turned onto the historic road. Close to his parents. A boon to the community.

All he wanted.

Yet when he looked at Faith, who was unblinking, unmoving, the victory felt hollow.

Chapter Thirteen

Faith managed to sit through the rest of the council meeting with her head held high, though she couldn't have said what was discussed beyond an update about the schoolhouse fire. The fire investigation team determined a tourist inadvertently started the blaze by flicking a smoldering cigarette out his car window, and now that the area had been cleaned up, the council voted to allow the land to be used for the restaurant next door to expand for patio seating.

After that, Faith found it difficult to concentrate, but the moment Mayor Hughes ended the meeting, Faith made a beeline to Tom, hand extended.

"Congratulations."

He enveloped her hand in both of his warm ones. "Thanks, Faith. I hope—"

"Tom." Elena slunk her arm through Tom's, breaking his contact with Faith. "The mayor wants a word with you."

"In just a minute, Mom."

"She's in a hurry, and you have papers to sign so we

can get into that shop and get to work. Faith understands you won fair and square."

Tom's dark brows knit. "This wasn't a game to be won, Mom. Faith and I both want what's best for the town."

"And it's clearly your store." Elena's tone was almost gleeful.

Faith had thought Elena didn't like her friendship with Tom because they were competing for the building. But maybe Elena was just straight-up mean.

Either way, it was not worth saying anything at this moment, except for one parting word. "Congratulations again, Tom."

She joined Angie and Chloe by the door and they took their leave. They didn't say much on their walk back to the antiques store, as if they understood Faith was holding it together until they reached the safety of the store. Fortunately, Angie had her key out to open the antiques store so Faith didn't have to show off how jittery she was by digging out her own key. Once inside the store, Angie rushed for the tea urn. "Here, honey."

Faith could hardly swallow the tea Angie offered. "I—I just can't."

"It's Earl Grey, though."

As if the flavor would help. Faith's throat was tight as a fist, trying to hold back a sob. "Thanks, but I need a minute."

Chloe came around Faith's other side. "You did a great job, really. Everyone was impressed by your presentation. I could tell."

The shop door swung open and Faith braced herself for customers, but it was Maeve who rushed in, lips turned down, arms extended. "My own husband voted for Tom's store. I'm sorry."

"No, Tom's store is a good idea." Faith pulled back and met her supporters' gazes. "It'll bring customers to all of our shops."

"But what about a museum?" Angie shook her head. "This town needs one, and I intend to write a letter to the council to say so."

"I will, too," Chloe said.

"You don't live here, so they won't listen to you, sugar bear," Maeve reminded Chloe. "It's a nice gesture, though."

The door opened. Kellan bore a sad smile for her. Nice of him to come by, but oh, Tom was right behind him, tie loosened, hair rumpled. What was he doing here? Shouldn't he be celebrating with his parents?

Everyone stared at him, but he only looked at her. "I'm sorry, Faith."

"Thanks, Tom. And I meant what I said. Congratulations."

He didn't look the least bit happy. "I didn't expect it to be unanimous. Or so fast."

"I would say that makes the outcome hard to dispute, then. This is what's best for the town." Even though she wanted a museum to be best, too.

Maeve reached out her hand to him. "Our Faith is a good sport, so I should do the same. Congratulations, Tom, and welcome to Main Street."

"Yeah, welcome," Kellan echoed.

"Thanks for being so gracious to me. All of you."

Faith picked up her cool cup of Earl Grey. She still couldn't drink it, but the bergamot fragrance was calming. So was the sight of Bettina peeking down the staircase. Little reminders God was with her and loved her, even on utterly awful days.

Chloe nudged Tom in the ribs. "We're discussing writing letters to the council stating our desire for a town museum."

"I'm going to write my letter today," Maeve said.

Angie's eyes brightened. "Maybe we should make it a petition."

"I'll sign it." Tom yanked off his tie and tucked it into his pocket, like he was full of nervous energy.

In fact, everyone seemed to be talking over one another now, as if they needed to do something to help Faith. It was touching, truly, but it was all starting to feel like too much. Like she needed some space. "It's okay, everyone. Really. God has something in mind, I'm sure."

"Of course He does." Maeve nodded with sympathy.

"But the way things are now, no letter or petition is going to get Mayor Hughes's support for a city-funded museum. That's the reason I decided to start my own in the first place." Faith set down her cup. "This just clearly isn't the right time."

"I don't know if it's the timing that's the issue." Kellan shoved his hands in his pockets. "I think it just wasn't the right place. Before the schoolhouse burned, you were talking about fixing it up, right? What if we built a recreation of it to house the museum in? All we need is a vacant lot."

Tom leaned against the counter. "It was too small for Faith's exhibits, though. We need a larger building."

Maeve crossed her arms over her ample midsection. "What about one of the new storefronts to the west? By the high school?"

"Or by the highway, to welcome visitors?" Kellan rubbed his chin.

"They're all great." Faith sighed. "But I can't work at those locations and here in the store at the same time. So maybe if we're going to have a museum in town, I need to back out of being a docent. It's more important that Widow's Peak Creek gets a museum than it is for me to run it, right?"

"Right," Chloe said. "But I don't like the idea of the museum in a strip mall. It needs to be downtown, in the historic hub. Which is why I think it should be right here." She circled her index finger, pointing around the room.

"Here? As in Faith's Finds?" Faith gaped. "There isn't room for the exhibits and my wares, too."

"No, you can't have them both here." Chloe folded her arms.

Tom's brow furrowed. "Do you mean, put the museum upstairs, and Faith could live somewhere else?"

Kellan shook his head. "No, the store can use both stories, just like I do at Open Book."

"But your second floor wasn't altered into an apartment, Kellan," Maeve noted. "The apartments above these stores are zoned residential, so that option is out."

Chloe grinned. "Not upstairs. I mean right *here*, where we're standing, and it wouldn't push out your stock, Faith, because your antiques store will go somewhere else."

"Move the store?" Faith had never considered such a thing. "But Main Street is the main tourist strip." As well as her home. She could live above the museum, of course, but how would she handle that and a store? It was the same dilemma she faced if she put the museum elsewhere.

Chloe leaned against the refurbished desk Faith had fixed up for Willa. "I know it's a lot, Faith, but thanks to this baby right here, you're going to need more room anyway. You've sold one of these renovated desks sight unseen. Well, unseen except for texted pics, anyway. But once others see this? Up close, so they can get a gander at the detail you and Jason put into this? And they will come to see furniture like this, by the way, after hearing about them through word-of-mouth and the website you need to set up. Believe me, you're going to need more space than you've got right now."

It was nice of her to say so, but Faith shook her head. "I doubt that."

Tom rubbed his chin. "You already know I agree with her projection, Faith. Vintage charm, quirky touches, modified for the modern consumer? You get a website, make a few more connections, and it could really take off."

"If it does, it's thanks to you and your idea." It was all she could think of to say.

He shrugged off her thanks. "It was an idea, but you ran with it. You're the one who had the vision and talent to create this desk, which is gorgeous, by the way. I'd buy it, if it wasn't already sold. In fact, I'm going to put in an order with you. Before you get swamped. Custom one-of-a-kind furnishings like this? Who wouldn't want this?"

Now he was just trying to make her feel better about her lousy day. She smiled anyway. "I appreciate your support, but I doubt I'll be swamped. It could be a while before these sell. If at all. And in the meantime, I'm not giving up my antiques store."

"You can have an antiques store anywhere, though, Faith." Chloe folded her arms. "And if you had a bigger store, you could sell your regular stock alongside your refurbished furnishings. And you should have it in the Bay Area, which is where the bulk of your buyers will be. I'm not ragging on small towns, but you know as well as I do the market is better for things like this in a larger, metropolitan area." She rapped on the desktop.

Faith's mouth went dry. "You want me to relocate?"

"Yeah." Chloe grinned.

Faith felt Tom's heavy gaze. What was he thinking? It was impossible to tell.

Chloe reached and shook Faith's arm. "You can stay with me until you get your feet underneath you. Won't that be fun?"

"What about the museum?" Maeve voiced one of Faith's thoughts.

"It's for the town, right? Faith just said someone else could run it, and this spot right here is as good a location as any."

She'd decided to trust God about the museum, hadn't she? Was Chloe right? Should she leave town and start over?

Okay, this was a little dramatic. Losing the property, discussing options… It was a lot. "I'm not going to make any decisions right now. This has been a long day and it's not even lunchtime."

No one laughed at her attempt at humor.

She decided to change tacks. "You know, we should celebrate Tom's new store. Will you have a grand opening party?"

"I haven't thought about it." He rubbed the back of his neck.

"You should. You deserve to launch your store in style. And I want to help with it."

"That's really generous of you, Faith. You're a great friend," Tom said.

Yep. That was her. Friend zone all the way. "It'll take my mind off things. Chloe's going home tomorrow, anyway. It'll be awfully quiet around here."

"I'll miss you, too, sis." Chloe hugged her for the first time since she'd come back to Widow's Peak Creek. "Move in with me."

"Oh, Chloe."

"It might be good for you to start over, if all the doors here are closed to you," she whispered.

She didn't just mean the museum. She meant Tom, too.

Faith had to wonder if her sister was right. Maybe staying here, with Tom as her neighbor, wasn't the wisest course of action when it came to protecting her heart.

The following Friday, Tom stood in the center of his store, a surge of pride swelling in his chest.

His store. The World Outside. God had been so good to him.

"You can see how it's going to look, can't you?" Ender walked past, tapping a screwdriver against his palm. "Now that the shelves are going in?"

"I can see it." And Tom loved it.

It had been nine days since he'd received the key to the storefront, and they'd accomplished a lot in that time. A new counter had been installed yesterday. Jason, from Sparky's, stood atop a ladder, installing track lighting above. They'd hired staff, stock had started to arrive, and in another week, the grand opening celebration would take place.

"Perfect, huh?" Ender dropped the screwdriver into the metal toolbox with a plink.

Tom's chest deflated. "Almost."

"I take it by your tone you're referring to Faith."

"Yeah." Tom moved behind his new counter. "I hate that this hurt her."

"Angie said she's been quiet. More than usual, anyway."

"The whole museum thing is upsetting. I want to help her, but I don't know how. When I dropped off my rental agreement, I spoke to the mayor. She confirmed there is no money for a museum, not for the space or personnel or obtaining new artifacts. Faith is right. It has to be private or it can't happen at all." If God wanted the museum, He'd make it happen, but it was beyond Tom how it would work out.

Faith seemed hopeful, though. At least she said she was. And she hadn't said a word about taking Chloe's suggestion that she move out of town. She clearly wasn't taking it to heart, to his relief.

"I'm blown away by how nice Faith has been through this," he said, buffing the countertop with a rag. "She made flyers for the grand opening. She's bringing them by tonight."

"Here?"

"No, the house. The kids have been asking for her, so I'm ordering pizza." *Asking* was not the right word, though. *Insisting* was more like it.

"Well, that's interesting."

Tom puffed out a breath at his friend's amused tone. "Don't do that, man."

"Do what?"

"Smile, like this is something it's not. There's nothing going on with me and Faith, okay? Not like with you and Angie. You know I'm focusing on the kids."

Ender's brow arched. "Does Faith know that?"

"She does." Tom pushed harder against the counter-top. It needed to sparkle.

"It's okay if you want to be more than neighbors with her, you know."

"We are more than neighbors. We're friends. Faith is such a good friend that she's helping me with the grand opening, and you know what? I'm going to help her with the museum when things settle down. That's what friends do."

"I'm not arguing with you there. But I think you two could be a lot more. You're allowed to love someone again, you know."

Tom was not going anywhere near the *L* word. "Do you mind picking up sparkling cider for the grand opening?"

Ender shook his head at the change of subject. "Sure. How many cases?"

Tom remained at the store until kindergarten pick-up and then worked on financials and stock at home until the doorbell rang at 5:30 p.m. "Miss Faith's here," Nora announced, followed by the sound of the front door opening. Tom hopped up and followed her, Logan and Roscoe outside to meet Faith.

"Hi, guys." Faith wrapped an arm around each twin and squeezed.

"How's Bet-teeny? We haven't seen her in ages." Nora took Faith's hand.

"She's fine. She says meow."

Logan cracked a half grin. "Tell her meow back."

"Will do."

A quick pat for Roscoe, and Faith joined them in the

house. Tom was the only one she didn't hug, which was… appropriate, wasn't it? Friends like them didn't hug.

Although the day before the city council meeting, he picked her up and whirled her in a circle, which was way more than a hug, but that was different. And it couldn't, wouldn't happen again. "The pizza was just delivered. Wanna eat while the food's hot?"

"Sure. I'm really hungry. But I didn't come empty handed."

He'd assumed the canvas tote over her shoulder held the grand opening flyers she'd made up. "What is it?" Logan hopped up as if it would help him look inside.

Along with a manila folder—the flyers, no doubt— Faith pulled out two plastic-wrapped bundles, one purple, one teal. "I saw how much you two enjoyed the kite at the daffodil spot, so I thought you should have your own. These are just like the blue one hanging in my shop window."

"Are they an-teek?" Nora snatched the purple one.

"No, they're new."

"Can we fly them now?" Logan tore open the plastic.

"First of all, how about, *thanks, Miss Faith*. And second, we're about to eat. But soon."

"Thanks, Miss Faith." His kids hugged her so hard she stumbled a half step back.

Faith met his gaze and grinned. "Hope it's okay I didn't ask you first."

"It's great. Really thoughtful." He should've remembered the whole kite thing, but the gift coming from Faith meant something special to the kids. And to him. His stomach warmed, watching them all.

Faith set her tote down by the couch. "Since the pizza's hot, I'd better wash up."

"Me, too." Logan pulled her free hand, leading her and Nora down the hall to the guest bathroom. Tom listened to their chatter and running water while he set the pizzas and a tossed green salad on the kitchen counter, along with plates. The table was already set with napkins, forks and water with lemon wedges for Faith.

After grace, they dug into the steaming pizzas. A few bites later, chatter started about their days. Faith dabbed her lips with her napkin. "Someone came into the store today looking for interesting teacups. She said it's a tradition in her family to give one to each girl when she turns eighteen. Isn't that sweet? But she's had trouble finding something unique for this particular granddaughter."

"Did anything work out for her?"

"An art deco piece, mint green. Really cool item." Faith helped herself to another piece of pizza.

"What's a tradition?" Logan picked a piece of sausage off his DeLuca's special.

"Something families do time after time or for birthdays or holidays." Tom stole Logan's abandoned bite of sausage. "Like it's a tradition for us to eat enchiladas on Thanksgiving instead of turkey."

"You do?" Faith smiled at his nod. "Yum."

"Eating pizza with Faith is a tradition," Nora noted.

Tom swallowed the sausage. "It's not quite the same thing."

"We do it over and over, and we all like it." Nora was insistent, and Tom didn't see the point in arguing that having pizza with a friend a few times didn't make it a tradition. Not that he couldn't get used to this. Time spent with Faith was fun for all of them.

The familiar tune of his cell phone ringtone interrupted Logan, whose mouth was open to speak. Tom hopped up. "Sorry. I'll silence it."

"No phones at the table," Nora explained to Faith. "Not since we moved to Widow's Peak Creek."

"Good policy."

Tom was about to silence it when he saw the name on the screen. It was after work hours, but he'd been playing phone tag with a product representative for three days. Wincing, he turned around. "Actually, this is kinda important. I'm sorry, do you mind?"

"Of course not." Faith shooed him with her hand. "Sometimes things like this happen," she said to the kids while Tom answered the phone.

He took the phone into the office so he could jot down notes, and when the call finished, a sense of satisfaction coursed through his veins. He was still grinning when he returned to the trio at the kitchen table. "Sorry, but that was a representative I've needed to talk to."

Faith set down her water glass. "What's the product?"

"Will you kick me if I say a rock climbing wall?"

"Very funny. You know that's not allowed."

"Yeah, yeah, but I'm keeping it a surprise. It's an interactive display, let's put it that way. Kids will love it."

"One of those big net things you hit golf balls into?" Faith guessed.

"Or bikes," Nora offered.

"We're selling and renting bikes, sweetie, but no, that's not the surprise. Nor is it a golf net." Tom leaned back in his chair. "You're just going to have to wait and see."

Faith lowered her crumpled napkin to her plate. "I know I was skeptical at first, but I'm glad you'll have something interactive for kids. Kids need wholesome activities and outlets."

Following the direction of her napkin, it dawned on him every plate was clear. They'd finished eating while he was gone. "Sorry, I thought I was faster than that."

"It's okay." Faith shrugged. "We'll wait while you eat."

It wasn't okay, though. Not to Tom. He ended up excusing the bored kids so they could examine their kites. "This is the sort of thing I swore I wouldn't do again."

"Devouring pizza like a college student?" Faith's delicate brows lifted.

"Handling business during off hours. Leaving the kids to their own devices."

"What am I, chopped liver?" Her lips twitched.

"You know what I mean. *I'm* supposed to be here one hundred percent with them."

"You took a business call that was sort of urgent. Grand opening is coming up fast. It's okay you handled it."

"I thought it wouldn't take me that long, though."

"A lot of things will take longer than you want them to, Tom. The store's security system will have false alarms, your cleaning service will quit, an employee will get sick and leave you hanging. It's all part of running your own business. Having to step away from your kids for a few minutes while you do doesn't make you a bad parent."

"It did in San Francisco." He stood and stacked the plates less gently than they deserved.

She followed him into the kitchen, carrying the salad bowl. "I wasn't there, but from what you've told me, this is totally different."

"How? Because I'm not traveling? I still wasn't with the kids just now."

"No, things are different because you're aware of how busy you are. Because you're paying attention. That's huge. You realize things will take you away from the kids on occasion, but it's not your everyday way anymore."

"What if it is?" He couldn't meet her gaze. "I'm accustomed to working all the time. Like, all the time."

Salad bowl on the counter, she faced him, hands on his shoulders. "Not since you've been back in town, you haven't. I've seen you, Tom. Leaving work to get the kids from school, being with them, loving them. It doesn't sound like the old Tom did that."

"Because I had Lourdes."

"And a totally different way of living, from all you've said. But that's changed. Tell me, do you have other business you could have attended to this evening?"

"Yes." *Loads.*

"But you didn't. You passed this test, don't you see? You handled one call and you came right back to your kids."

Her hold on his shoulders hadn't lessened. It was emphatic, not romantic, but it burned all the way down his arms. "Are you sure, Faith?"

"Yes. I wouldn't say it if I didn't mean it. I know what a struggle this has been for you."

He shut his eyes. "Thank you."

God was working in him, then. He wasn't entirely out of the woods when it came to keeping work from creeping into his family time, but he'd improved enough that someone noticed his efforts.

And unlike his parents, Faith wasn't chastising his failings. She was encouraging his victories.

Her hands slid away and he opened his eyes. She was

still within the radius of his arms, if he were to reach out for her. Still near enough for him to see the green flecks in her eyes, the movement in her throat as she swallowed.

Four pounding feet approached from the living room, making Faith move to the sink, turning on the water. She'd squirted soap into the sink when the kids burst in. Nora's eyes were wide and her hands spread, making emphatic gestures. "We want cookies."

"Cookies? What? We don't have cookies," Tom teased, glad his voice sounded normal after being in close proximity to Faith.

"Yes, we do." Logan hopped like a pogo stick.

"We have to clean up first." Faith dunked the salad bowl in the soapy water. "Come on, many hands make lighter work."

"What does that mean?" Logan's nose scrunched.

Faith turned off the faucet. "The more people pitch in, the faster we get finished."

"I don't want to touch the plates." Logan grimaced at the smear of tomato sauce on Nora's used plate. Then he sputtered as a splotch of soap bubbles hit his neck.

What on earth?

Faith held soap bubbles in her palm and puckered her lips, like she was about to blow some on Nora. Nora squealed and ducked for cover behind Tom.

"No, Faith, no." His hand went up. But he was smiling so broadly it hurt his cheeks.

"I promise not to get any on the floor." She sounded so sweet, saying it. "Just you."

He lunged, pinning her arm to his chest, getting soap all over his T-shirt in the process. "You want a little *clean* fun, eh?" He dipped his hand into the sink and swiped a palm-full of bubbles on her head.

He let her go and dropped a blotch on Nora. Then something cool and wet trickled down his spine.

Faith's belly laugh was a new sound. "You needed some, too, Tom."

He feigned outrage as he swiped the back of his neck. "I invite you to pizza and this is what happens."

"Can we wash Roscoe?" Logan alerted Tom to the fact the dog had joined the chaos.

"He just had a bath."

"And there are dishes to do." Faith fisted her hands on her hips and adopted a serious expression that didn't match her laughing eyes. "Come on, guys, who started this craziness, anyway?"

"You did." Nora poked her in the thigh with a soapy finger.

"You're right. And I'm going to clean it up. Tom, where are your rags? I don't want anyone to slip on a slick floor because I'm a weirdo."

"I'm a weirdo, too, because I liked this." Logan took one of the towels Tom pulled from a bottom drawer. "I want to soap fight again."

"Maybe this summer we can have a water fight outside. If—well, never mind."

What did that mean? If? If what? If she was still here this summer? Was she thinking of taking Chloe up on her offer to move to San Francisco?

He couldn't read an answer in her eyes once she dropped to the floor, mopping the tiny blob of soap bubbles by the oven.

"Faith?" Tom took her hand and lifted her to her feet. As she looked up at him with questions in her eyes, he didn't want to ask her what she meant by that "if" any-more. He wanted to pull her into his arms and—

Kiss her. Like he'd wanted to do for a long, long time now.

Fortunately, Roscoe bumped into him, breaking their eye contact and his stupid train of thought. He had to take a few good breaths before he could talk again. "Let's do these dishes so we can have cookies, yeah?"

He couldn't do that again—think about kissing Faith. Nothing, nothing would wreck their friendship faster than him giving in to temporary feelings. He had to shove that dangerous thought right out of his mind.

Besides, She might be leaving Widow's Peak Creek to focus on her furnishing business. Maybe there was more to it than that, too. Like she resented him for get-ting the space she wanted for her museum.

He couldn't ask her about it now, not with the kids listening in. Instead he tried to focus on making the rest of the evening a pleasant one.

He did pretty well, too, as he praised the flyers she'd made for him, and they discussed the grand opening while the kids watched a cartoon movie. Faith was all in, helping him with the party. Food, timing, everything. She was much better at this type of thing than he was, but he couldn't help but notice an underlying sadness in her eyes.

Was it because she'd lost the store to him? Was it hurting her to help him, which she did out of the kind-ness of her heart?

They joined the kids for the rest of the movie, and both kids slumped against Faith on the gray couch. Even Roscoe lay at her feet.

It didn't hurt Tom's feelings that they chose to snuggle

with her. It was nice to have a good female role model in the kids' lives.

Faith left after the movie, and the kids bathed and got into their pajamas. They had separate bedrooms, but their custom was to switch rooms for story time. Tonight, they piled on Logan's twin bed, surrounded by stuffed animals, with a book. When Tom read the final page, he asked the usual question.

"What should we pray about tonight?" He set the book on Logan's nightstand.

"A mommy." Logan snuggled a plush superhero to his chest.

"Not just any mommy." Nora nodded sagely. "We want Miss Faith."

Tom couldn't speak for a moment. Faith? Their mom?

"Guys, we've talked about this. Our mommy is in Heaven."

"And we want a new one. Miss Faith."

Logan nodded. "We've wanted her since daffodil day."

Tom's brain sparked with a memory. That day, Faith tripped, and they'd pushed him to help her the whole way back. He'd assumed they were concerned about her hurting her knees again.

But his sneaky kids had been trying to get him and Faith together.

His kids had blindsided him, but he should have noticed their machinations. Paid better attention. His parents had warned him about the kids getting too attached to Faith. He'd shrugged it off, maybe because he was getting attached to her, too.

He wouldn't analyze the emotions wreaking havoc in his chest. Instead, he took the kids' hands. "Let's pray, okay?" He wouldn't chastise them for their choice of prayer request. But he couldn't discuss this anymore with them right now.

Once both kids were tucked into bed, Tom staggered to his bedroom, rubbing his face. What was he going to do?

His kids wanted Faith as their mom.

Tom was in no position to give his kids a mother, much less date. His kids didn't need a woman stepping into their lives. They needed him.

He'd promised his parents. Himself. God.

Besides, he'd sensed Faith was harboring sadness tonight. Not in the way she spoke or acted, but he'd noted it in her eyes. She had to be hurting over losing the store to him. And if she did indeed move away to live with Chloe? That would devastate the kids.

It didn't take much prayer to figure out what he had to do. He had to step back from his friendship with Faith, before the kids grew more attached.

Before he did, too.

It felt like his heart cracked down the middle, but he had no other choice.

Chapter Fourteen

"Miss Faith!" Logan and Nora rushed into the antiques store on Tuesday, fresh from kindergarten judging by their backpacks.

"Hello." Faith stopped finagling an oversize chair into place and extended her arms for hugs. Their presence seemed to fill up an empty reservoir inside of her. She glanced up at Tom, who lingered in the doorway, before returning her attention to the kids. "How was school?"

"Good." Nora pulled something from her pink backpack. "Another thank-you note!"

"I wrote it all this time," Logan pointed.

"Except for my name," Nora corrected. "I drew my purple kite and a cat."

"I drew the big boulder by the creek." Logan gestured to the gray lump in the corner of the card.

"I love it all. And you're most welcome for the kites." Without thinking about it, she dropped kisses on their heads.

"What are you doing?" Logan looked around.

"Moving things around, boring stuff. I should just wait for Miss Angie to return from lunch to help me. But anyway, I sold another fixed-up desk today." Her gaze met Tom's. "One of Chloe's friends is a designer. She thinks a desk like the one I sold to Willa at the Cordova would be a *fresh seasonal look.*"

"That's awesome, Faith." He smiled, but he didn't step farther into the store. He must be super busy today, getting ready for the grand opening. It was in less than two weeks.

She wouldn't keep him, then, but she had to give credit where credit was due. "It's all thanks to you and your idea."

Tom shook his head as his kids meandered to the corner of the shop where she kept the cabinet of historical artifacts. "Ideas are a dime a dozen, but you're the one who did the work and added your own creative spin on it. Your sister was right. There is a huge market in the city for your work. Maybe you should visit Chloe and check out options."

Faith moved closer to Tom so they didn't have to raise their voices across the store. "I have been considering them, and you'll be glad to know I decided to get a website, like you suggested."

"Good. It'll help." Tom fixed his gaze outside, like he was watching for a delivery truck. "But I was also thinking you should look into catering to your initial customer base. Both Willa and this friend of Chloe's are in larger cities."

It took a moment for her to form words around the lump clogging her throat. "Are you suggesting I leave Widow's Peak Creek? Move in with Chloe?"

He met her gaze then, his expression sad. "I want you to have every opportunity, Faith. That's all. You lost the museum, and I don't want you feeling like you're missing out on anything else."

That hadn't been on her mind five minutes ago. Now she was starting to feel deflated as a day-old balloon.

"I've got to get back to the store." Tom beckoned his kids with a wave. "It's going to be a busy several days if I'm going to be ready by the grand opening."

Still reeling from his remarks, Faith struggled to keep her tone even. "Anything I can do?"

"We're set, thanks." His smile didn't look quite authentic.

"If I can watch the kids at all—"

"Mom and Dad are on the few things I can't get out of right now. Thanks, though."

Faith's spirits weren't just deflated now. They were decimated. "I'm here if you need me, okay?"

"Sure." He wasn't looking at her. "Come on, guys, we've got to go unpack boxes."

"Can Miss Faith help us?"

"Miss Faith has her own store," Tom answered. "See you around, Faith."

"See you around." *Around where? The neighborhood? Church?*

I know he's busy, Lord, but that was like we weren't friends at all.

Clearly, something had changed, and Tom wanted to put some distance between them now. She didn't understand why or what prompted the change with him, but she had no choice but to respect it.

Nevertheless, it was shocking how much it hurt when he and the kids walked out of the store.

Faith didn't feel much better about Tom, or life in general, when the day of the grand opening celebration arrived clear and hot almost two weeks later. Summer came early to gold rush country, but the heat brought tourists, which was good for Main Street.

For the first time since she'd opened Faith's Finds, Faith's mind wasn't on the benefits of the high season. It was on the desk she was finishing up in the store's back room, screwing knobs into the drawers. The knobs were all the same size and resembled delft-style tiles, blue painted on white, but each bore a different scene, which would go over well at Willa's, in Faith's thinking. One final twist and she set down the screwdriver. Done.

Now what would fill her mind, since the distraction of the desk was finished?

The lack of a museum? Or the lack of Tom in her life?

He hadn't so much as waved at her through the window for days. At church the past two Sundays, he and the kids left quickly with his parents, before she could greet them. Sure, he'd been busy getting ready for the grand opening of The World Outside. She'd heard workers hammering all day long through their shared wall.

But Faith suspected Tom's avoidance had more to do with him not wanting to see her, rather than his being busy. She must have really done something to upset him the other night at his house. The messy soap bubbles? Talking him down from his frustration with himself?

Whatever it was, she couldn't help but interpret his statement about her "looking at her options" in the city through a troubling lens. It sure felt like he had grown to dislike her so much, he preferred her to leave town.

Should she consider leaving? This was her home, but maybe she needed to let go of her Widow's Peak Creek dreams, like this shop and the museum, and open herself up to new ones. Like the desks.

Is that where we're heading, Lord? A new dream You've yet to show me?

Somehow, the idea of running a new antiques shop with space to showcase altered furnishings didn't feel right. But for so long—her whole life, it seemed—she'd yearned for support from her family, for a sense of belonging that she'd previously only experienced here with her grandparents.

She'd felt it with Tom and the kids, too, but it turned out that hadn't been the sort of belonging that lasted.

Now, she and Chloe texted almost daily. Maybe God wanted her to continue that restoration work by being in the same town as Chloe.

She exited the workroom in the back of the store and found Angie folding lace curtain panels at the counter, humming to herself. Faith came up behind her and looked out the window at the busy foot traffic on the street outside—people heading to Tom's grand opening party.

"I'm thinking of going, Angie."

"To the party? I thought we weren't going until five."

Even though Tom was avoiding her, she'd decided to drop in to see the kids. She'd missed Logan and Nora so much, which made Tom's avoidance all the more painful.

But that wasn't what she meant when she approached Angie.

"I mean going to San Francisco. To visit Chloe."

Angie's look was sharp. "For a second there, I thought you were going to say you might move in with her, like she wanted."

"I have to be honest, I feel…unsettled right now."

Angie's demeanor changed to one of anguished sympathy. "Oh, honey, this has to be killing you, going to a party to celebrate a building you wanted for the museum. It's awful."

"Thanks, Angie, but it's okay. I'm sad, sure, but it is how it is. I'm happy for Tom and the kids."

"I thought maybe you handled the situation so well because you and he were—well, becoming an item. Ender could see it, too, but something's changed in the past few weeks. That has to hurt."

"It doesn't feel great, but the only thing we set out to do was handle our conflict like adults."

Angie rolled her eyes. "It's all over your face, honey. You like him."

She'd better change her facial expression because she did not want those feelings to show. Or to even exist. She'd known that Tom wouldn't date. And she didn't want to be with someone who could cut her off like this, anyway. End of subject.

A laugh carried through the wall between her and Tom's store. "It's after four. Should we just close up shop and go over there?"

"It has been quiet in here since the party started. Sure." Angie flipped the door's open sign over.

Faith tidied a few things before running upstairs to pat Bettina and freshen up—a quick swipe of lip gloss, a run of the comb through her hair. One side had lost the curl she'd given it this morning, so she shoved the unwavy bit behind her ear and grabbed her beaded purse.

"Ready?" Angie waited downstairs, her makeup reapplied and her hair glossy.

"Let's go." Faith locked the shop up behind them.

The doors to Tom's store were wide open, allowing the happy noise of multiple conversations to spill onto

Main Street. Faith fixed a cheek-aching smile in place and crossed the threshold.

The place was packed with people. Kellan sipped what looked like apple cider from a plastic cup, and Maeve eyed a sign proclaiming rental prices for bikes and kayaks. Childish shrieking from the back of the store made Faith spin. "What in the world?"

"A rock climbing wall," said a familiar voice. Tom's. He held out cups of bubbly cider to her and Angie. "I told you I was going to have one."

"You did, indeed. Well done." It wasn't a real rock wall, mounted to the wall like the one she'd climbed on in Sacramento. It was a gray plastic mountain-shaped play structure maybe seven feet tall, with footholds and a few openings to cling to, set atop a cushioned mat. Logan, Nora and two kids she didn't recognize clambered over it. Ender stood guard, grinning like one of the kids.

"Excuse me. I've got to go say hi." Grinning, Angie slipped away.

"Remember when we had pizza a while back and that vendor called? This was what we were talking about," Tom said.

It was awkward, standing here after not speaking for a while. His cologne didn't even make her knees weak. The only thing she felt was a nervous hollow ache in her gut. "Well done. And congratulations, Tom. The store is amazing."

"You really like it?"

Meeting his gaze hurt. "I do. And look at how many people are here. The grand opening is a success in every way, I'd say."

"I appreciate your help with the flyers and everything, Faith." Tom glanced at her lips. "I should probably mingle."

"Yeah, of course." Faith turned away and sipped her juice. Tom was the host of this party, but he could've spent more time talking to her if he'd wanted to.

Why should he? They'd set out to be neighborly after their argument in front of the kids, and they were civil now. Mission accomplished.

So was her mission to show up at this thing. Finishing her juice, she walked toward the playset so she could tell the kids hello before returning home.

Angie and Ender weren't supervising the kids anymore. Tom's parents hovered at the edge of the mat, grinning ear to ear until they saw her.

The kids spied her so it was too late to go somewhere else. "Hi, guys." She hugged a sweaty Nora first, then Logan, once they dropped from the playset. "Good evening." She didn't offer her hand to Elena or Roberto this time, and they didn't extend the courtesy, either.

Logan tugged on her hand. "Faith, watch me."

So she did, clapping for him when he reached the top of the playset, then for Nora. "You're king and queen of the mountain."

"Mount Santos," Nora announced.

"I like it." Roberto grinned.

"I like the whole store." Maybe if Faith assured Tom's parents she was glad for him, they'd loosen up a little bit where she was concerned.

"Grandpa, I'm thirsty," Logan called.

Roberto joined the kids to search out juice just as Mayor Hughes, elegant in one of her tailored blazers, sidled alongside Faith and Elena. "Isn't this wonderful?"

"It is." Faith clutched her empty cup.

"Just what the town needed." Elena probably hadn't intended her comment to be barbed, but it hit home anyway.

Mayor Hughes patted Faith's arm. "Sorry about your museum, Faith, but I just don't see it as a priority for my constituents. Resources would be better spent elsewhere."

She couldn't hold her tongue any longer. "It's too bad, though. Your father-in-law donated several artifacts to me, including photographs of your husband's ancestor founding Hughes Park. Until there's a museum, there's nowhere to display them."

The mayor shrugged, as if completely uninterested. "Since you have no need of them without a museum, feel free to leave them at city council when you go, then."

"I beg your pardon?"

"Aren't you moving to San Francisco with your sister?"

"You are?" Elena's shoulders and frown relaxed.

The mayor knew about Chloe's offer? "Nothing's been decided yet."

The mayor patted her again. "Sounds like a great opportunity for you. It'll be good for Tom, too."

She had a million questions, but only one popped out of her mouth. "How so?"

"Then he can open that wall between your stores. Double his capacity so he can put in a putting green and some other interactive displays. City council thinks it'd be a great draw to Main Street."

Elena's thin penciled brows rose. "Oh, marvelous."

Faith didn't trust herself to say much of anything, so she settled on a quick "Excuse me." Where was Tom?

Laughing it up with some guy in a red plaid shirt by the fishing rods, that's where he was, like he didn't have a care in the world. He must have recognized something in her expression because he excused himself from Mr. Red Plaid. "Something wrong, Faith?"

"So *you* want *my* store now?"

"What?" His low voice matched hers.

"Mayor Hughes just told me all about your plan. City council is all for it. So is your mom, by the way."

So much for wanting to stay friends. So much for even being neighborly.

She should've kept her distance from the start. It would have saved her a world of heartache.

Tom's brain couldn't keep up with her words, and the loud buzz of conversation around them made this all the more difficult to process. "Will you come into the office? Please?"

"As long as you plan on explaining, sure."

Explaining what, exactly? He'd clearly missed something. He slipped with her through the mingling guests until they reached his office, a cramped space made more stifling from the unpacked paper boxes wedged between the empty bookshelf, the sleek slate-colored couch and his modern desk. Once Faith stepped inside, Tom shut the door behind them. "What's going on?"

Faith stopped in the center of the room, arms folded. Her white blouse and pale blue pants were soft and sweet looking, but she bore the fierce expression of a Valkyrie. "The last time we talked, you encouraged me to visit Chloe. Is that because you wanted me out? So you can expand into my store?"

"I don't want to expand into your store. The thought never crossed my mind."

"Hasn't it? Then why is the mayor saying the council is thrilled about a putting green in Faith's Finds?"

"I don't know, but it has nothing to do with me. I suggested you look into your options because I want you to feel fulfilled, Faith. I know how hard it's been on you, not being able to start a museum. And I want you to be happy, so that's why I said that." He did want her happy, with all his heart. "It has nothing to do with expanding into your store."

She didn't seem appeased. "So that's not why you've been curt lately?"

He could say the store kept him busy, but the truth was he'd been rude. For a purpose. To protect his kids.

"I'm sorry, Faith."

It was all he could do.

It was obvious, though, she wanted more. Deserved more. But he couldn't give her anything, so he leaned against the desk waiting for her to talk.

She was still in the center of his office, her eyes damp with pain. Pain he'd help put there. As much as he hated himself for it, he couldn't reach out the way he wanted to. Couldn't give her comfort. Couldn't even tell her the kids had asked for her every day, because that would make things worse.

All he could do was let her be angry at him. Angry and sad.

She glanced at the ceiling. "I was thinking, literally ten minutes before coming here, that maybe I should leave town. Go be with Chloe, like you said. For a visit, and then maybe permanently, because things aren't working out for me here."

Tom bore some responsibility for that. "If I hadn't come back, you'd have had your museum by now."

"I'm not so sure about that. The mayor would've found something else to go in here, or limited the museum's lease so she could kick me out as soon as something else came along." She shoved a loose strand of hair behind her ear in a frustrated gesture. "I need to accept that and look into donating the artifacts in my possession to a gold rush–related museum elsewhere."

"I promised to help you, though. I still think there has to be a way to have a museum here."

She shook her head. "Maybe it's time I stop asking God to bless what I want, and look at joining in what He's already blessing. It seems like the furniture adaptations are my future, not the museum, so…"

The office door swung open, and his mom glared at him, then Faith. Faith forced a fake grin. "Sorry to keep you from your guests, Tom. Pardon me, Elena—"

"Are they in here with you?" Mom craned her neck.

"Who?" He pushed off from the desk.

"Don't joke. Logan, Nora, come out, now."

Tom's blood iced. "They're not here."

"Are you sure?"

Faith gasped and looked behind the couch.

"Logan? Nora?" He peered behind the stack of paper boxes by the bookshelf. There was nowhere else to hide in the office.

Fear, sharp and black, descended over Tom from head to toe.

First Lourdes. Now his children. He'd stopped focusing on them and now they were gone.

Chapter Fifteen

Panic mounted in Faith's chest, squeezing her lungs, as she hurried after Tom into the store, but she pushed at it before it took hold of her. Gaze darting everywhere for the two sweet faces, she forced her thoughts to fix on facts. "The kids went with your dad to get a drink."

Elena's hands fluttered. "They came back after you left and they heard me ask Mayor Hughes about Faith leaving town. I didn't think it would upset the kids, but Nora started crying. I looked for a tissue, and when I found one, they'd gone."

"You didn't think it would upset the kids." Tom turned back, his face contorted with fear. "They love her, Mom."

"I'm sure that's not it, *mijo*. They're playing hide-and-seek or something."

Tom shook his head and skirted the store, going from group to group. "Have you seen Logan and Nora?"

Faith didn't much want to engage Elena, either. Not when the kids were unaccounted for. Not with the way her heart seemed to have leaped out of her body, leaving her cold and empty.

Since Tom was searching the store, she ran outside.

No dark-headed kids. She peeked into her empty store, checked the alley and tried the street door to her apartment in case she'd left it unlocked, even though she knew she hadn't.

She moved on, fast, peering in the shop windows on their side of the street. Every store was closed, except for the eating establishments, but quick check-ins told her they weren't there. Back on the sidewalk, she cupped her hands around her mouth. "Nora? Logan?"

Angie burst from The World Outside, brow furrowed. "Find them?"

Faith shook her head, swiping her damp eyes while she was at it. "Where could they have gone?"

"Roberto is driving the route to Tom's house right now in case they're walking there—see, there's his car." Angie pointed as a silver sedan turned out of the corner parking lot. "Ender's calling the sheriff, and Kellan and a few others are searching around back. They can't have gone far. It's only been a few minutes."

Maybe they couldn't have gone far, but what if someone had taken them? Just because Widow's Peak Creek was a safe community, didn't mean it wasn't possible. Faith couldn't give voice to the awful thought. *Stay positive. Trust in the Lord.*

"Oh, Lord, please help us find them."

When she and Angie reentered the store, Tom looked up, his agonized expression lifting a fraction when he saw her. She shook her head, and he buried his face in his hands. The few guests who remained at the party looked inside the display tent, the clothes racks and the stock room at the back.

"We're here for you, Tom." Maeve lowered her hand to his forearm.

"Thank you." His voice was anguish itself.

She wanted to wrap her arms around him, promise him they'd be found, assure him he wasn't losing his kids the way he'd lost his wife, but it wouldn't help. Tom had borne so much, and expected so much from himself. He achieved—or overachieved—to prove to his parents, and himself, that he wouldn't make the same mistakes he'd made in San Francisco. Yet, now the kids were out of his sight, his hands.

And she was so scared, she wanted to retch.

Hand to her stomach, she bent to peek under the cloth-covered refreshment table. It would have been her choice of hiding spots as a child. "Not here, Lord. Where are they?"

She was praying aloud, but she didn't care if it seemed odd to anyone. Up and down rows of merchandise, she searched, praying. "Draw my eyes to them, Lord. Or someone else's eyes. You know how much this family has been through. Please show these kids how loved they are, no matter where they are or how they're feeling."

She gripped the side of the empty playset, clinging to a blue plastic foothold as if it could bear her weight. Her mind raced, scrounging to think of potential hiding spots. "Lord, show us. Show us."

Something inside the playset moved. Just a little, fleeting as a mouse. Faith dropped to her knees and peered in one of the tiny openings. A brown eye blinked at her.

Nora's.

She didn't know she cried out until Tom came alongside her. She didn't remember Nora scooting out, just that she was in her arms, smelling like sweat and the plastic of the playset, crying hard.

"Sweetheart, we were so worried." Now that her heart

was beating again, she kissed the top of Nora's head, then relinquished the little girl to Tom. Faith then ducked to look in the tiny hidey-hole for Nora's twin. "Logan?"

"He's not here," Nora managed between hiccups.

Faith's heart stopped again. "Where is he, Nora?"

"I don't know. He was running away."

Faith's heart resumed pounding, hard and fast in her chest. "Where did he go, honey?" Tom's tone for his daughter was gentle, but Faith could nevertheless detect a note of panic in it.

"I don't know." Nora resumed sobbing.

Tom stroked Nora's hair, even as his fearful gaze met Faith's.

She had to find Logan. Now.

The store had been thoroughly searched, which meant she might have missed him when she looked around Main Street earlier. She ran back out into the late afternoon light.

Running away. To a six-year-old boy, that could mean anything from the bus stop to a spot in his backyard.

Which had a creek behind it. What if he'd gone to the creek and fallen in?

Roberto was on his way there. She could ask Elena to text him to be sure he looked in the yard, but he'd do that, wouldn't he? Other people she recognized from the party were getting in cars, assigning themselves and others areas to search, including the creek trail.

But the creek didn't just run behind the Santos home. It also ran through town here. Faith ran south, past the schoolhouse site, over the footbridge, past the restaurants, turning at the old church and entering the grassy expanse of Hughes Park. Ahead was the big boulder, a place of fascination for Logan. He wanted to roll his toy cars off it. He wanted to climb it. It was the biggest rock in the world, right?

"Logan?" Her call was just shy of a scream, but fighting off her panic was proving harder and harder. "Logan, honey, are you here?"

There was no reply, but a small orange sneaker stuck out from behind the boulder.

"Logan!"

He scooched around to see her. She burst into tears and gripped him in a ferocious hug. *Thank you, Lord. Thank you.*

His little chest heaved from crying. "Why are you moving away, Miss Faith?"

Oh, Logan. She kissed his dark hair and squeezed even tighter. "I'm here, sweetheart. I'm here. I—"

She couldn't finish when someone tugged him from her arms. Elena. Faith had no choice but to relinquish Logan to his grandmother, but immediately, Elena handed Logan to Tom. Someone must have seen Faith running and followed. It was a good thing they did—now Tom was freed of the terror he must be feeling, knowing both kids were safe. Tom's eyes shut as he gripped his boy to his chest, murmuring loving words.

It was beautiful, this reunion, an answer to prayer that the kids were safe. She reached for Elena. "I'm so glad."

Elena stepped away. "Thanks for your help, Faith."

Faith's mouth went dry. Clearly Elena didn't want her here. This was not her family. Elena was making sure Faith knew it, too.

Wiping her eyes, she slipped away.

Thank You that they're safe, Lord. Thank You.

Her heart was full and breaking at the same time.

* * *

Once the kids were in bed that night, Tom allowed himself to fall apart. As much as he could with his parents over, anyway. He flopped onto the loveseat, kitty corner to his parents on the sofa, and rested his elbows on his knees, hanging his head.

"I thought I'd lost them."

Mom moved to sit beside him and scratched his back with her long fingernails. "After Lourdes died, we all realized how fast things can happen. Today was a fresh reminder."

Tom understood the implication, that he had not been an attentive father today. "I should never have taken my eyes off them."

Dad sighed. "It's not your fault, Tom. Your mother and I said we'd watch them while you attended to customers, remember?"

Mom stopped scratching. "Customers, yes. But you shouldn't have hid in your office with Faith Latham, Tom."

Tom bolted to his feet. "That's enough about Faith, Mom."

"What?" Mom's eyes bugged. "I haven't said anything wrong."

"You didn't say you want her to move away?"

"Not in so many words, no, but just think what it would mean for your store if she did."

"I doubt it's my store that's foremost on your mind. You're more interested in keeping her away from me, but she's our friend, Mom. The kids care about her. They hid because you and the mayor let loose some unfounded rumor about her leaving town. The kids' affection for her is mutual, too. Did you see Faith's face when she found Nora? Did you see her crying when she was with Logan?"

"Pushy, if you ask me. They're *your* children and *our* grandchildren. If anyone comforts them, it should be us."

"Faith didn't cut in some imaginary line to hug the kids. She found them." Tom rubbed his temple. "My point is, Faith cares about Logan and Nora."

"Okay, so?" Mom pursed her lips.

Dad rubbed the back of his neck. "Come on, Elena."

"What, Rob?" She shot him the look of death.

"Faith was borderline-hysterical when we couldn't find the kids," Dad said.

"We were all scared."

"Not like that, Mom." Tom started pacing. "Faith is good to them. Good for them. And while I promised you I wouldn't get involved with a woman who would distract me from the kids, Faith hasn't done that."

"You're involved with her, then? You admit it?"

"Not like that. But I—"

Tom stopped pacing. He hadn't named it, in his thoughts. Hadn't admitted it to himself.

But this was no small thing happening to him.

"I appreciate all you've done to help with the kids. I couldn't work or—or have survived the past several months without your support. The kids and I needed you. Still need you."

"But?" Dad gestured that Tom should go on.

"I've spent the last two weeks avoiding Faith because of the way my feelings have grown, to keep my promise to you and to myself, and because the kids asked me to make Faith their mom. She doesn't know, and I changed the subject with the kids, but at that point I put distance between us."

Mom muttered something about them having a mom. And a grandma.

"I put all this distance between me and Faith, Mom, but it hasn't changed how I feel. She's important to me. To the kids. You saw proof of that today." Breathing a prayer, he met his mother's gaze. "How can I be distracted loving a woman who cares about the kids as much as I do? Who makes me a better dad?"

Dad stood up, eyes suspiciously damp. "You love her, son?"

"I do." It felt amazing to admit it at last. "And I hope you can trust me from here on out."

"Tom, this is crazy." Mom rubbed her temples.

Tom dropped to his mom's side. "I love you so much, Mom, and I appreciate how hard you've worked to help and protect me and the kids, but I don't like how you've treated Faith."

"What's she said?"

"Not much. But she knows you want her to leave town. Whatever the mayor was talking about, me expanding into her store, it's utterly false. And it hurt Faith. I have a lot to do to make things right with her, but you need to know where I stand with her. If she's willing to forgive me, I'm going to do my best to convince her not to go to San Francisco unless that's what she really wants to do." He'd hate it if she left, but he wanted God's best for her. Whatever it was.

"I've been mean to her." Mom sniffled. "I'm sorry. I just didn't want her getting in the way of you focusing on the kids."

"I know, Mom." He'd pray for full reconciliation between her and Faith, who was the one who still needed to hear Mom's apology.

"Maybe there's still hope for a museum here." Dad stretched out his legs, crossing them at the ankles. "Granted, you need a spacious place, and you have to consider things like security, cleaning, that sort of thing. Seems like all the shopkeepers on Main Street have experience with those things. Can you ask them for ideas?"

Something clicked in Tom's brain. "Maybe that's it."

"What is?" Mom's eyes dried up somewhat.

Tom glanced at his watch. Too late to call Maeve, but first thing tomorrow?

"It might not work. But I have to try."

To put a museum in town. And try to keep Faith here. Close. Where he could show her how much she'd come to mean to him.

If it wasn't already too late.

Chapter Sixteen

Monday afternoon saw a steady stream of customers at Faith's Finds, mainly tourists who took advantage of the fine weather to visit the area. A few mentioned renting bicycles next door at The World Outside. Good for Tom. His business was off to a healthy start.

Not that she'd seen him. She'd hurried from church on Sunday, waving to the kids, but that was all. After what happened when she found Logan, she wasn't ready to talk to Elena. Or Tom, but he was so busy chatting with Maeve that he didn't seem to notice her hasty retreat.

Since then, she'd kept up a near-constant internal dialogue with God about everything. Should she check in on the kids? Should she stay put in town or should she join Chloe? Would she ever get over Tom?

It might be easier to move past her feelings for him if he wasn't her next-door neighbor. Thinking of him literally ached.

Then again, she loved running an antiques store in her hometown. Today was a perfect example, because the family perusing the store right now—a balding dad, a mom with a graying bob, plus two lanky teens who'd mentioned they were homeschoolers—seemed interested in almost everything in the store. Their sense of joy warmed her aching heart.

"Mick, look at this." The wife beckoned her husband to show him the curved silver in her hand. "My grandma had one just like this."

"What is it, Grace?" Mick pushed his glasses up his nose.

The teens looked up from the vinyl LPs. "What'd you find, Mom?"

"A baby spoon, or training spoon. Is that right?" The woman looked to Faith, who'd been dusting the buffet.

"Exactly. Designed for a child to curve her fingers through the handle."

"I ate off one of these at Grandma's house until I was probably twelve, because I thought it was so cute. I wish I had it. This sure makes me think of Grandma." Grace looked wistful. "She was such a fun lady. I wish you'd known her. All of you."

"Why was she fun?" The daughter took a turn with the spoon.

"Well, for one thing, she never turned down a chance to play with me," Grace began.

Faith wandered back to the counter, smiling. *This* was why she'd opened the store. The stories that accompanied historical objects could bring folks together. Objects like that little spoon, since it set off a chain of memories for this woman, and now she was sharing those stories with her family.

Thanks, God, for reminding me why I do this. Whether it's here or elsewhere, I know You'll be with me. Please show me if You want me to move. I'll go wherever You want, even though I confess it'll hurt leaving my home and friends. And Tom and the kids. I wish I didn't care about them this much, but I have to trust that You have a purpose for it, even if it's a reminder to place You first. You have a plan, and I want to submit to it, wherever You take me.

The woman laid the spoon on the counter with a soft thud. "I'm definitely buying this, but we aren't finished looking around. I may find something else we can't live without."

"Take your time." Faith pulled out a sheet of tissue paper to wrap the spoon in.

"These buildings are original to the town, right?" The husband glanced up at the ceiling.

"They sure are. This particular building was a seed and feed. An opening right over there connected it with the livery next door, which is now The World Outside. The two businesses were owned by relatives back then."

"We ate lunch at Del's Café. What did that start out as?"

"A bathhouse and barber shop. I still have the scissors the first barber used, too. They're over in the display case over there."

"It's like a little museum in here," the daughter said. She and her younger brother wandered over to look at the cases.

"Is there a map for a walking tour?" Grace peered over the counter as if she'd find a pile of them. "Or is it at the welcome center?"

"We don't have a welcome center, or a map, but those are great ideas." She'd always thought of distributing a map like that at the museum. Maybe she could still do it here, though. It wouldn't be hard to sketch something up, labeling the historic buildings.

Angie slipped in the open front door, returning a few minutes early from her break. "How are things?"

"Great. You've got more time, if you want it."

Instead, Angie tapped the tissue-wrapped bundle with a buffed fingernail. "What is it?"

"A silver training spoon."

"Which one?"

"The one with the bird etched on the handle. They're still shopping, though." She tipped her head at the family, perusing the display cabinets. "Super sweet folks."

"Why don't you take your break? I'll ring them up when they're ready."

"It's okay. I've got this covered."

"Actually, you're about to be too busy to help customers." Angie stared at her. Hard.

This was beyond weird. "What's going on?"

Rolling her eyes, Angie took Faith by the shoulders and turned her so she faced the door.

Tom—his full lips parted in a hesitant smile—stood in the open threshold. "Hi, Faith."

"Tom. Hi. How are the kids? Are they okay?" It blurted out before she could stop herself.

"They're great. Really. They'd love to see you later, if you have time."

"I'd love to see them."

"They're at the store."

"Oh, you mean *now*. Okay." No wonder Angie was pushing her to take a break. She must have been next door, visiting Ender, and known Tom would be coming. "I'll be back in a minute, Angie."

"Take your time." It almost sounded like a command.

Faith preceded Tom out the door and turned left toward his store. The bright afternoon sun blinded her, and she had to cup her hand over her eyes.

"Actually, wait." Tom's voice pulled her up short. "Do you mind if we talk without the kids first? It's important."

Nodding, she turned around and they started walking at a leisurely pace, super slow. The speed didn't matter, though. All she cared about was getting a full update on the kids. "So Logan and Nora are okay? Saturday was awful. I feel so bad about it."

"I guess Kellan mentioned Chloe's idea that you move in with her to someone who told the mayor, and from there, the rumor spread. I assure you, I didn't know. Nor did I tell the mayor I wanted your storefront, because I don't. But it devastated the kids."

"I am so sorry about that. Did you tell them it's all bunk?"

"No, because I wasn't sure what you'd decided, but I did tell them it would be okay. Anyway, thanks for finding them. Both of them."

"I didn't do anything special. I just happened to be looking down at the right angle to see Nora. And I was thinking how much Logan likes the big boulder, so I thought I'd check."

"You know them really well, Faith." Tom stopped walking and faced her, and oh, boy, his citrusy smell waved over her and she had a hard time not staring at his scruffy chin and cheeks, so close she could touch them. "They care about you."

"I care about them, too."

"I know." He smiled as if the knowledge made him happy. "Come in here for a second."

They were at Apple a Day, the store by Faith's Finds. "Do you need vitamins or something?"

"Something, yeah." He held the door open, so she went in, blinking as her eyes adjusted. It smelled like vitamin powder and fruit. "I want to show you something. Right there." He pointed at the back corner that was stocked with herbal teas last time she was here. Now it was empty.

They walked past Gwen, the redheaded proprietor, who greeted them with a nod as she helped a customer. Tom took Faith to the empty corner, placing her in front of it like he was going to put her in an old-fashioned time-out. "This, Faith, is stop number three in the Widow's Peak Creek Museum Walk."

"The what?"

"In 1850-whatever—I can't remember, you'll have to help with that part—this building was used by the assayer. So right here, where you're standing, we're going to put a museum-quality display of artifacts that the assayer used. Scales, photos, maybe a little gold, and a document explaining what the assayer did. Come on."

He took her hand and tugged her out of the store, but her brain was still in the back corner. "I'm super confused, Tom. Can I talk to Gwen about this?"

"Later. Let's go to stop number four." He took her into Del's Café, grinning like Logan when he was asking for more dessert.

The aromas of soup and coffee filled her nostrils as Tom pulled her to a stop in the front of the café, right by the register. George, the manager, rubbed his hands together. "Isn't this neato?"

"Isn't what neato?" Faith whispered.

Tom pointed to the bare wall. "George and Sandy are putting a cabinet here to display some of the tools the barber used in here, since this was the barbershop and bathhouse."

Her brain scrambled to catch up. Stop number four on the—what had he called it? "A museum walk?"

He squared his shoulders. "Until Widow's Peak Creek gets a museum, the Main Street businesses are all participating in a museum walk. Each store has committed to displaying artifacts from the building's original business. They're dedicated to keeping the items secure and clean, and to serving as docents for those particular items. If that's okay with you, of course."

Faith's hands went to her mouth. It was difficult to speak, much less untangle her words. *All the stores? Everyone?*

"Why are you doing this?" she managed at last.

"Because we need a museum, and we all want to help people learn about this town until one can be established the way it should be. Come on. See what everyone's done. They can't wait to show you."

"I can't wait to see."

Faith had to jog to keep up with Tom's long excited strides. Sure enough, every store they visited had cleared space for displays. Maeve was so excited about the dental artifacts going into her yarn store she'd already ordered a special cabinet.

"That's not all." She took Faith by both hands. "If the mayor doesn't think there's enough funding for a museum, she either hasn't studied the budget well or she's plain biased against one. So I've decided we need a new mayor. I'm going to run in the next election."

Faith hugged her. "You'd be amazing at it, museum or not, Maeve."

"Until then, we're all excited about Tom's walking museum idea. Isn't he a genius?"

"He's—"

She couldn't finish once she met his smiling gaze. He was something, all right.

Tom took her hand again. "Wait until you see the others."

Claudia at Angel Food Bakery, once the town stationer, showed them where she'd set her display cabinet. Emerald's Restaurant, originally a dry goods store, planned a presentation of old cans and a poster listing 1850s prices for goods. Kellan grinned when they entered the bookstore. "No room for an anvil like the blacksmith once had here, of course, but a few authentic smithy tools can go in this cabinet. I'm expanding my selection of local history books, as well."

Faith gave him a half hug before Tom drew her outside, across the street.

As Tom said, each store was participating, from Neopolitan's Ice Cream Parlor to DeLuca's Pizza. Instead of crossing the street back to Tom's store, however, Tom turned her around the way they'd come. "Let's go to the park for a minute so I can tell you the rest. Don't worry about your store. Angie's fine."

"What about your store? And the kids?"

"Ender is running things, and Mom is watching the kids play on the rock climbing thinga-ma-bob."

Elena knew Tom was with Faith? *Huh.*

She had other things to think about right now, though, as they walked southward toward the old church, and beyond it, the park where she'd found Logan. "This is amazing, Tom. I'm overwhelmed. And confused. I didn't think anyone else was supportive of a museum, but now everyone on Main Street is hosting mini-museums?"

"You've taught us all about our heritage, Faith. Me, the kids and every shopkeeper on Main Street. I wanted to consult with you before I set up my display, though. I was thinking of hanging old tack on my wall to commemorate the livery. Do you like that idea?"

"It's wonderful. And you are, too—I mean, thank you."

"I'm going to add historic trail tour maps and the occasional guided hike to the mines, too." They stepped onto the walking path that followed the creek. Ahead, the park sat lush and shady. "Let's go to the boulder."

"Sure." Maybe he wanted her to show him how she'd found Logan.

It was cooler here, beneath the large shady oaks. Faith knew her goose-pimpled flesh wasn't all about temperature, though. It was about Tom's gift of the walking museum. "Thank you, Tom."

"It's not the museum you want, but it's better than my dumb idea of using the schoolhouse, don't you think?"

"Much."

"A lot of things are better than I dreamed. Like coming home." He slowed to a stop beside a bench near the boulder, and by unspoken agreement, they sat. "I wanted to run away from my past, and when I started taking the kids to church, I realized God was sending me home so I could start over. Seems an odd choice of places to go when you don't want to relive the past, but this was where I needed to be. Thanks to Him and you, I was reminded again and again that while I need to trust Him for my future, I also need to trust Him with my past. I'm not defined by my mistakes, but He also cares about the legacy I leave behind. Family and spiritual, both."

"I trusted God with the future of the museum and it's turning out better than I dreamed, because it involves so many people. And keeps you next door so your kids are cared for the way you wanted them to be." Faith shifted on the cool wood bench slats. "Wherever God leads now, I'm going to try to do a better job of trusting Him."

"Is He leading you to move to San Francisco with Chloe?"

"Honestly? The past few weeks I've felt…rootless. Friendless in some ways. Which has been hard, because Widow's Peak Creek was the only place I've ever felt I belonged."

"And I changed that, because I avoided you?"

He admitted it, which hurt anew. At least he was honest. "Yes. Plus the mayor's attitude."

"My mom didn't help, saying the things she did to you. Yeah, she told me. The thing is, though, my parents are right."

"About you not dating." She fixed her gaze on the mossy-dark creek. "I get it, but I thought we were friends."

"Not regular friends." When she looked back, his eyes had darkened to deep pools of ink. "My parents saw what I couldn't admit. That my kids loved you. That I want more than friendship with you."

Oh.

"I had to step back for the kids' sake, as well as ours, because the truth is, I don't want to date. When the time comes, I want a marriage. Not a short-term relationship. Does that make sense?"

"You care about me, but the timing is wrong. Are you

asking me to fade out of your lives or wait?" She'd never asked such a bold question before.

"I'm not saying it well." He reached out and gently took hold of her chin. "I love you, Faith. So much. I want to be with you. But not to casually date. To be with me and build a future with me and the kids. I'm not trying to scare you, telling you all of this, but you should know my intentions. I come with a lot of baggage, though. Twins and a dog and a workaholic tendency I'm scared to death of falling back into. If you aren't interested in a bigger commitment down the line, if you don't feel the same way about me that I do about you—"

She had to stop him right there. "I love you, Tom."

"You do?"

Couldn't he hear her heart pounding so hard and loud it was about to explode out of her chest? "You and the kids. I've missed you all so much it hurts."

His hands gripped hers, warm and fierce. "The future won't be perfect, but I'll be by your side, if you let me. Me and the kids."

All she ever wanted. "But what about your parents? They'll disapprove."

"Actually, they've come around."

Really?

"I can't guarantee the kids won't destroy any more of your store displays, and I'm sorry about that." His gaze lowered to her lips.

"I could use a little more chaos, I guess."

He didn't smile at her tease. Nor did he remove his gaze from her lips. "You really love me?"

"Yes, Tomás." So much she could marry him here and now on this bench.

It would have to wait, though, because he cupped her

jaw, kissing her thoroughly. Like she'd never imagined a kiss could be, and she was in a dazed stupor when he stopped.

"Sorry that was in public. I didn't mean to embarrass you."

His voice quavered, which made her feel smug. Faith could get used to this.

"Not embarrassed, but if anyone saw us, they'll talk, so we'd better hurry and tell the kids."

"Yeah?" His face lit up.

"Yeah." She stood up, clutching his hand. "We haven't had our pizza tradition in a few weeks."

"No, we haven't."

"And we definitely need to celebrate with the kids tonight." The Walking Museum and being together. So, so much to celebrate.

For the first time, Faith was running into the future. And with Tom by her side, it felt wonderful.

Epilogue

Two months later

Faith entered her apartment, stepping into utter chaos.

The blue rug askew on the foyer floor. The kitchen abandoned, even though marinara sauce sputtered out of the pot, messing up her stove. The garlic bread in the oven smelled perfect. Much longer and it would burn.

She and Chloe had been gone all of what, twenty minutes? However long it had taken for them to run for fixings to put on the ice-cream sundaes Tom insisted they needed for dessert tonight, leaving him and the kids to finish cooking dinner in her kitchen.

It had been weirdly uncharacteristic of him, sending her out like that, even after she offered to take them all to Neopolitan's if he was in that big of a mood for ice cream.

But he'd insisted, so she and Chloe ran out to buy a half gallon of vanilla, chocolate syrup and whipping cream. Faith set the canvas bags of groceries down on the counter and checked the garlic bread. Yep, golden brown on top, but it would be black if she didn't rescue it now. She donned an oven mitt and took the pan out of the oven, and then she placed a lid over the marinara. "Where is everybody?"

"Bettina's not in the bathroom," Nora yelled from down the hall.

"Bettina's missing?" Stripping off the oven mitt, Faith went through the kitchen to the living room, where Tom was on his hands and knees, head behind the couch. "Maybe she went down to the store."

"I doubt it. The door's been shut since you left." Tom glanced up at her before shuffling to look under the adjacent chair.

"You sure?" Chloe joined the search party, peering around the bookshelf.

"Yeah, I'm sure. She was here."

"She's not playing in the shower curtains," Logan shouted.

Faith fought a rising sense of fear. Why would they be looking so hard for her cat if nothing was wrong? "Is she sick or something? What happened?"

Tom stood and took firm but gentle hold of her shoulders. His inky-dark gaze met hers, calming her as only he could. "She's fine. The kids want to play with her, that's all."

That didn't exactly constitute an emergency, but Faith would pitch in and join the hunt. "She's probably sleeping somewhere." Much as she preferred to stay in the circle of his arms all day, she pecked Tom's delicious-smelling cheek and reached to open the guest room door. "Maybe she found a quiet spot under Chloe's bed."

"Don't go in there!" Chloe ran to lean against the door.

"Why?" Faith didn't remove her hand from the knob.

"Because it's a mess."

"It's always a mess, when you visit."

"But Tom and the kids don't need to see that."

This was weirder than weird. Faith was about to push her way into the guest room, but a snuffle drew her around. Nora stood in the hallway behind them, her eyes wide with worry. Logan peeked out of the bathroom, chewing his lip.

Faith's heart turned to mush. "You guys are really worried, huh? Let's go look under my bed, okay? Chloe can check under her bed away from our prying eyes." She glanced at her sister. "Then maybe you can put the ice cream away?"

"Sure." Chloe snuck into her bedroom like it held a top-secret conclave of world leaders inside.

That must be one huge mess in there.

Leading the kids into her room, Faith crouched at the foot of her double bed, nudging the blue-striped bed skirt up enough for them to peek beneath it. Sure enough, Bettina lay in what Faith called her "Cleopatra" pose, back legs curved to the side, front paws together, her posture both regal and relaxed.

"See, she's fine." Faith lowered the bed skirt. "Let's allow her to go back to sleep."

"I think we should get her out." Nora's voice held a tinge of panic.

"Are you worried because she's in a tight space? It's okay, honey. Cats like to be cozy."

"She should be cozy in the living room," Logan insisted.

"Daddy?" Nora called.

Something woofed at the same time. Not from the street below, but the next room. Faith stood up, straining to hear. Nothing. Maybe Chloe had moved a chair and it sounded like a woof or—

There it was again. A woof she knew quite well by now. "What's Roscoe doing here? What's going on?"

Several things happened at once. Tom appeared in the threshold, his face utterly devoid of expression. Nora slithered beneath Faith's bed and shooed Bettina out the other side, where Logan caught her and handed her to—Tom?

Enough was enough of this weirdness. "Tom, is that Roscoe?"

"I'll take care of it. Here." He handed the cat to Faith. Bettina's name tag jingled against the metal clip on her collar while Faith rushed to the guest room door, which now stood wide open. The guest room was now vacant, but the sounds of dog breathing and shuffled steps came from the living room.

Faith was there in two steps.

Roberto and Elena, holding Roscoe by a leash. Faith gaped. "Hi." It came out more like a question.

"Hello, Faith." Roberto grinned.

"Did you see Bettina?" Nora popped to her tiptoes.

"Of course I did, I'm holding her. I—"

Faith looked down. The jingling noise hadn't been Bettina's name tag against the metal clip of her collar. The noise came from her name tag striking an addition to her collar, a gold circle with a stone on it.

A solitaire diamond ring.

She gaped at Tom.

With a nervous lick of his lips, he took Roscoe's leash from his dad's hand. Roscoe, she now saw, wore a pale blue bandana with writing on it.

Will you marry my dad?

Faith's stomach bottomed out. This was happening. Really happening, right now. "Tom?"

"The dog isn't asking on my behalf, exactly." Tom dropped the leash and reached for Faith, his warm hands on her shoulders. "But this is about more than you and me. The kids had input in this proposal, and we decided to include everyone in our families. Pets and people."

"All of us," Elena said. And by her smile, Faith could tell she meant it. Things hadn't been perfect with Elena since she and Tom started dating, but Elena had apologized for the things she'd said to Faith. Together, they'd worked toward a healthier relationship. Elena's words now felt like a blessing.

Faith could only spare her a thankful glance, however, because it was proving impossible to look away from Tom. Being this close to him did crazy things to her insides, and now she understood why he'd dressed in a button-down and khakis and taken some time with his appearance.

"You shaved."

"It's a special occasion." He glanced at her lips. Then lower, at the cat. "Do you mind if I take the ring off her so we can put her down?"

She held up the cat while he unfastened the cat collar, his fingers trembling. Then the ring slid off and she set Bettina on the couch.

Tom moved back, lowering to one knee. "Faith Rachel Latham, I came back to Widow's Peak Creek to build a home for my kids. But we—I—can't imagine that home without you in it."

Faith's hand went to her mouth.

"You're in my heart, my every waking thought, my prayers and my plans. I want to open the sealed door between our stores so I can see you when we're working. I want to grow together in a godly family relationship and see what God does with us. I love you with every fiber of my being. Will you do me the honor of being my wife? Of joining our family?"

"Say yes," Nora urged. A chorus of shushing followed.

Faith's hands lowered to his. "I spent so long focused on the past, Tom. But now I want to focus on the future. And the present. With you. You're my love. You and Logan and Nora. Yes, of course, I will marry you."

The ring was warm when he slipped it on her finger, but she didn't look at it overlong because he was on his feet and pulling her into his arms for a hug that lifted her off her feet, followed by a kiss that might have stopped her heart if it had gone on a moment longer.

But then the kids were with them and she enveloped them in a long, fierce embrace. *Lord, I am so blessed You and Tom consider me worthy to help raise them. Thank You for giving me this family. For giving me Tom.*

"Can we eat now?" Logan rubbed his stomach.

"Yes, *mijo*, we can." Elena retreated into the kitchen. Within minutes, they were filling their plates, the apartment alive with the sounds of forks clinking plates and happy chatter. Tom and Faith lingered behind the others, held together by their gazes and interlocked fingers.

"I love you," he said.

"I love you," she echoed. He was hers, for now and always.

Past, present and future.

* * * * *

Dear Reader,

Thank you for joining me in Widow's Peak Creek. The town may be fictional, but bits and pieces of it are inspired by real California towns settled during the gold rush, which started in 1848. The whole area is rich in history and scenic beauty.

Like Faith, I sometimes find comfort in the certainties of the past, but at other times, I'm like Tom, yearning for a clean slate. Writing this story reminded me that no matter how painful or uncertain our times may be, God is Lord of the past, present and future. His grace is sufficient to bear us through the messy unknowns we face. He is faithful and loving!

I thank God for His help as I wrote. I also owe thanks to my family; my parents; my editor, Emily; my agent, Tamela; Debra Marvin; encouraging friends; and to you, dear reader, for supporting Christian fiction.

I'd love to connect with you! You can find me on Facebook (susannedietzebooks), Twitter, Instagram and Pinterest (susannedietze), and on susannedietze.com, where you can sign up for my newsletter for news, recipes and other lighthearted stuff. Until then, may the Lord bless you and keep you.

Blessings,
Susanne

WE HOPE YOU ENJOYED
THIS BOOK FROM
LOVE INSPIRED
INSPIRATIONAL ROMANCE

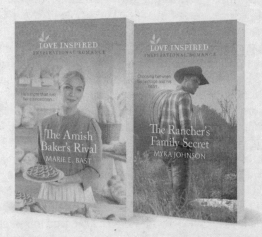

Uplifting stories of faith, forgiveness and hope.

Fall in love with stories where faith helps
guide you through life's challenges, and discover
the promise of a new beginning.

6 NEW BOOKS AVAILABLE EVERY MONTH!

SOMEONE TO TRUST
North Country Amish • by Patricia Davids
Esther Burkholder has no interest in her stepmother's matchmaking when her family visits an Amish community in Maine. Deaf since she was eight, she's positive a hearing man couldn't understand the joys and trials of living in a silent world. But Amish bachelor Gabe Fisher might just change her mind...

HER FORBIDDEN AMISH LOVE
by Jocelyn McClay
After her sister's departure to the *Englisch* world, Hannah Lapp couldn't hurt her parents by leaving, too—so she ended her relationship with the Mennonite man she'd hoped to marry. Now Gabe Bartel's back in her life... and this time, she's not so sure she can choose her community over love.

CHOOSING HIS FAMILY
Colorado Grooms • by Jill Lynn
Rescuing a single mom and her triplets during a snowstorm lands rancher Finn Brightwood with temporary tenants in his vacation rental. But with his past experiences, Finn's reluctant to get too involved in Ivy Darling's chaotic life. So why does he find himself wishing this family would stick around for good?

HIS DRY CREEK INHERITANCE
Dry Creek • by Janet Tronstad
When he returns home after receiving a letter from his foster father, soldier Mark Dakota learns that the man has recently passed away. Now in order to get his share of the inheritance, Mark must temporarily help his foster brother's widow, Bailey Rosen, work the ranch. But can he avoid falling for his childhood friend?

A HOME FOR HER BABY
by Gabrielle Meyer
Forced to sell her bed-and-breakfast, Piper Connelly's happy to stay on as manager—until the pregnant widow discovers her former high school sweetheart, Max Evans, is the buyer. While Max has grown from the boy who once broke her heart, is giving him a second chance worth the risk?

AN UNLIKELY PROPOSAL
by Toni Shiloh
When Trinity Davis is laid off, her best friend, Omar Young, proposes a solution to all their problems—a marriage of convenience. After all, that would provide her much-needed health insurance and give the widower's little girls a mother. And they'll never have to risk their bruised hearts again...